Prologue

The air turned cooler as the sun slowly went down as Paul and his three closest friends hiked up the New Hampshire Mountains. When the Abenaki Indians lived on the mountains long ago, they called the mountains 'Ndakinna' meaning "*our land.*" The main mountain which Paul chose to climb was hidden deep in the middle of the White Mountains. It's been chill fully known as Dark Mountain. The shadowy peak earned its name from town's people living at the edge of the mountain who were inspired by the absence of sunlight on the northern side. Abutted by two other mountains stretching high into the sky, the ensemble resembled a baby in its mother's arms. Dark Mountain, it's been said that it holds the most vicious curse in history.

It's said that the evil curse had been cast upon any white man who would put their hands on the Ancient Emeralds, would die a frightening death. No one knows when the curse was made, or why the curse was done, or if it's even real? The newer generations of the town's people are unaware of the evil curse, but some of the older townies remember, or perhaps will never forget. They fear it will once again be awakened, as it did twenty five years ago on April Fools Day.

Paul's mother told him the story of the evil curse, how the Indian's owned the land, and how the Ancient Emerald's were the eyes of the Dark Mountain Phantom. He never believed his mother's story but he always remembered the tale, and wanted to explore the mountain anyway. She told him many have hiked the mountain, and many have never returned. The eerie feeling Paul gets every time he thinks about the mountain made him more and more anxious to go up and find out for himself.

Finally, high school was over, and college in the western part of the country was just a couple of months away. Paul wanted to take that weekend trip he's been dreaming about, and explore Dark Mountain to see if all the stories were really true, or were they just…..

Paul and his friends were dropped off by Shauna's mom on the south side of the mountain. They headed up the mountain with everything they could possibly think of, and then some.

Paul remembered his mother saying she didn't want him to go, then he remembered her also saying, You're a grown man now, just be careful. He walked out of the house with every intention on coming back in two days hoping he'll find what he's been dreaming about, or just having one last good time with his best friends before real life got in the way.

They listened to the whistling of birds, the strange sounds of the perpetual wild, and breathing the clean mountain air as they walked away from the old car. Paul remembered when he was a young boy; a black man in his late eighties told him that on a warm quiet day when the wind blew across the mountain just right, you can hear a chain saw a hundred miles away. Paul never understood why the old man told him that or what the reason behind it was, but he always admired the way he said it.

He pressed his hand against a large pine tree, and looked back at his friends with a smile. He thought about his future and what his life will bring him, money, knowledge, experience, happiness, or maybe nothing at all. There's only one way to find out, he thought.

He looked through the trees towards the peak of the mountain, and breathed a lasting breath before they started hiking up the mountain. Strangely enough he saw an old rusted sign nailed to a tree that read. '*Stay on the trail'*. He looked down at the ground and noticed there was no trail, or even any resemblance of one.

The Legend of Dark Mountain
BY ANDREW P. LEBEL
1.

Friday Night

The sun went down across the mountain as the crickets began to sing into the night. Without warning there was loud laughter echoing through the forest as an owl turned its head.

"Tell us another story Paul," Shauna said squeezing his arm with affection.

"No!" Stephanie shouted. "Your stories are much too scary Paul. I'll never get any sleep in these creepy woods,"

"Come on Steph, it's only a story!" Mitchell laughed cracking open another one of his cheap-tasting beers.

Paul looked around his circle of friends with his big brown eyes flipping his long bangs over his head, and stroked the beginnings of a goatee on his chin. He smiled a bit as he looked at everyone, flipped his bottle cap into the fire, and then put his arm around Shauna. He squeezed her tight as he took a quick swig of his beer to clear his throat.

Everyone sat there keeping warm from the crackling fire when Paul began to tell his so-called version of the haunted story, Legend of Dark Mountain. Everyone became silent when a faint sound of a howl came over the ridge just as Paul began to tell his story.

"The moon was stuck behind the clouds eager to shine through. The town's people were scared of what lurked in the Forest of Dark Mountain. They say the mountain comes alive on nights when the moon is full. The animals run to hide, and the birds fly away as fast as they can. No one has seen the horror it holds, and some say the evil steals the young,"
Mitchell quickly swallowed the last of his beer, and popped opened another one as he listened on.

"It feeds on the living, and leaves a trail of blood to where it drags the rest of the human remains," Paul was getting into his story as the night became darker, as the fire simmered down. He could see his friends were listening deep, and seeing in their eyes their imagination was taking them away.

Stephanie was the quiet one trying hard not to listen as she tightly covered her ears. Her imagination got the best of her as she started to weep with fear. Mitchell looked over at Stephanie wiping her eyes, and shook his head with disappointment as he took another swig. He was tall, thin, and egotistical. He's had this thing for Stephanie since they were in the fifth grade, and always admired her personality, but most of all he loved the way she smiled because it made him feel good inside.

Shauna, a petite girl with a dark tan, athletic figure from being a varsity swimmer, baby blue eyes, and long natural blonde hair. She hated Mitchell with a passion, and thought he was trying to own her best friend Steph. She can't stand the fact that he never lets her out of his sight. She watches him with disgust every time they're together, and fumes inside as she sees the shit her friend puts up with. In some sense, she wants to find something against him so Stephanie would finally smarten up and get rid of that bastard once and for all. She wished Steph would find someone else to have fun with, and also get treated better. But that's her opinion.

Paul told his stories, and everyone knew he told them well. He wanted to be a professional writer and hoped that someday his break would come, and he would get something published. His English teacher said his ability wasn't imaginative enough, and he should think about becoming a laborer, or a machinist of some sort.

Mitchell stood up and walked into the darkness. He stood next to a tree as he relieved him self looking around the trees glancing back at the campfire. He could still hear Paul telling the story but only in broken words.

Suddenly he heard a strange noise close by as his thoughts went through his mind of what was lurking in the night. He imagined it was the Dark Mountain monster walking through the woods. He pushed himself to finish feeling somewhat scared, wetting the front of his boot. He dragged his foot on the dirt to get rid of the wet stain as he headed back to the campfire. He sat down picking up another beer, and looked over at Stephanie with her eyes tightly closed and her fingers still pressed tight in her ears.

"Jesus Christ Steph!" He shouted nudging her and interrupting Paul's story.

"What!" Stephanie screamed back. "I told you I don't like scary stories!"

"Mitchell, what the hell is your problem? Leave the girl alone!" Shauna shouted at him.

Mitchell swallowed the beer faster than a bird can fly, then crushed his beer can into a thin saucer, and flung it into the night. He quickly grabbed another beer from the cooler and violently cracked it open, purposely spraying Stephanie in the face. Stephanie sat there quietly in anger wiping the beer off with the bottom of her shirt.

"One of these days asshole you're gonna get what's coming to you," Shauna told him.

"Paul, tell your ball and chain to shut the hell up," He said and took another swig of his beer.

"Mitchell stop, you don't need to show off around us," Paul said calmly and glared deep into his eyes.

Mitchell knew Paul was serious as they stared at each other in silence. He swallowed his beer as fast as he could, crushed it with his foot, and quickly reached for another one. He felt the liquor starting to go to his head and slipped off the log. He smashed his hand against the ground tipping over Shauna's bottle of Jack Daniel's wine cooler. Everyone sat there and watched him as he dragged himself off the ground reaching for another beer. Shauna started to laugh. Paul still had a serious look on his face. Mitchell wiped the dirt off his hand and noticed his wrist was bleeding.

Stephanie got up and walked away and crawled into her tent hoping no one would say anything to her about her so-called boyfriend. Shauna got up and crawled in with her and gave her a big hug in silence. All Paul wanted to do is punch Mitchell as hard as he could, but he figured with all the beer he'd been drinking, he wouldn't feel a damn thing. He stood up, and poured the bucket of water on the fire still glaring at Mitchell. He took off his shirt, crawled into his tent and lied down on top of his sleeping bag. He heard Mitchell cough a couple of times, and heard the girls whispering of how much of a jerk Mitchell was being.

"Goodnight Shauna!" Paul shouted in somewhat of an attitude, and waited for her reply.

"Goodnight Paul," she replied back. "Goodnight asshole," Shauna shouted to Mitchell.

"Goodnight bitch!" Mitchell shouted back at her hearing his own voice echoing across the night.

Mitchell sat on the log and crushed the last of his empty beer can. He closed his eyes for a moment and listened to the sounds of the forest. His head was spinning like crazy and felt himself fall against the ground backwards off the log. He crossed his arms, and passed out on the ground.

Silence fell over the camp as Shauna stuck her head out of the tent looking for Mitchell. She stood up, and wrapped a thin blanket around her naked body. She quietly walked out of her tent, tip toed by Mitchell, and slipped into Paul's tent where he was still awake but his eyes were gently closed. She uncovered herself and cuddled against him feeling his warm skin against hers.

Stephanie was awake, and saw Shauna leave. She prayed Mitchell wouldn't enter her tent looking for some extra pleasure-filled excitement. She held the flashlight tight to her hand, and hoped she wouldn't have to use it against his head. She relied on Shauna to be there for her since they were always the best of friends, or perhaps more like sisters.

Shauna took on the job after Stephanie's mother died from cancer when she was eleven years old. She felt she needed someone to protect her from life, and guard her from abusive men like Mitchell, but gave her enough room to breath, and hopefully she would make up her own decisions about them. Stephanie knew Shauna was always just a step away if anything ever did happen.

Saturday

That morning Paul and Shauna woke up early to get ready for the day. Shauna quickly snuck back to her tent and noticed Stephanie was already up and out. She was trying quickly to throw her clothes on, when Paul quietly stuck his head in and startled her.

"Christ Paul," she shouted.

"Sorry babe," he said chuckling.

"Stephanie is gone. Is she outside somewhere?" she asked.

Paul looked around the camp, and didn't see her anywhere. "She's not out here. Maybe she went skinny dipping in that small water hole we passed just over the side of the mountain," he said trying to be funny.

"Stephanie wouldn't take her clothes off in front of the mirror," she told him being sarcastic then jumped into her jeans.

"Well then let's go find her. I'm sure she's close by,"

Paul took his head out of the tent and waited for Shauna to finish, and then realized Mitchell wasn't around either.

"Oh shit," he said thinking of the worst.

"What's the matter?" she asked sliding out of the tent.

"Mitchell's not here either,"

"Shit," she said as thoughts of Stephanie lying dead in a ditch somewhere went through her mind. "You don't think…"

"No, I think maybe they went for a walk to talk things out," he told her and wondered himself if Mitchell went on a rampage killing her overnight.

"I hope so. He's been a real asshole to her lately," They started walking to find their friends.

"Do you think maybe we should split up? We can search more ground that way," she suggested.

"I'm sure we'll find them soon enough. Let's go down near that water hole, maybe they're skinny dipping?"

They walked back down the mountain, and saw some movement through the trees. They hurried down and saw Stephanie holding on to Mitchell with all of her strength, who had obviously had slipped and fallen over a steep cliff.

Paul dropped to his chest looking down at the bottom cliff, and quickly grabbed a hold of Mitchell's coat. He yanked on him as hard as he could and dragged him up from the edge. Stephanie was breathing heavy, and crying uncontrollably. Shauna reached around Stephanie and held her tight until she could calm herself down.

"Mitchell, are you okay? What happened?" Paul asked still holding onto his coat.

"I was walking along with Stephanie," he said as he took a deep breath. "I stepped on a rock and slipped. I slid down the hill and grabbed hold of a small root over the edge. We were walking up there, and then I landed down here," Mitchell took another deep breath.

Stephanie stopped crying long enough to agree with his story, and put her head back down on Shauna's shoulder.

Paul helped Mitchell to his feet, and again looked over the edge to see how far down the bottom really was. "Let's go back to the camp, and get cleaned up so we can head out. I want to hike some serious ground before it starts to get dark again," Paul ordered.

Mitchell carefully leaned over and looked down over the edge. He realized Stephanie had saved his life from not letting him go when the root pulled out of the ground. He looked down at his hand and saw that he was still holding onto the root with a vise grip. He tossed the root down and walked over to Stephanie with a smile and gave her a big hug. "I'm sorry for being such an asshole to you lately. It won't happen again," he told her.

Shauna listened to his so called apology. She knew sometime down the road he was going to be back to his old asshole self again.

2

Paul, Shauna, and Stephanie stopped and sat on a fallen tree waiting for Mitchell to catch up, since he was the only one who was out of shape and struggling to hike up the mountain. Paul took his backpack off and laid it down on the ground. They saw Mitchell still struggling hard to walk up the mountain out of breath, and dragging his feet. Suddenly they saw Mitchell trip over a rusted barb wire fence left on the ground, fall, and then slide on the leaves down the mountain bouncing off small trees. He landed against a huge rock with a split in the middle.

Paul quickly ran down, as Stephanie and Shauna dropped their backpacks, and ran down the mountain with Paul to see if he was okay.

"Mitchell!" Paul shouted. "Are you alright?"

"Yeah, I think so. My backpack stopped me against the rock."

"Jesus, Mitchell you okay?" Stephanie asked panting.

Shauna stood there catching her breath, and wondered how many more times they'll have to rescue Mitchell from his stupid clumsiness.

"Yeah, help me take this friggin backpack off so I can stand up," Mitchell told them.

Stephanie and Paul unclipped the straps, and helped him take his arms out, as he rolled himself away from the rock. He put his hand down on the ground and pushed himself up. In the process, he accidentally cleared away some dirt from a buried rock, which had some sort of Indian writing on it. He wiped more of the dirt away, and tried to read what it said. Paul looked down at the rock, and saw the ancient Indian writing.

"What the hell does this say?" Mitchell asked looking at the strange writing.

"*Pkwedano majignol pamabskakil,*" Paul said out loud, and then suddenly the rocks slowly cracked open letting an inhuman stench escape through the opening.

Everyone covered their mouth and nose, and stepped back from the rocks to breathe the fresh air.

"I guess it means open the friggin smelly rocks?" Paul said with his hand still over his mouth.

Mitchell cautiously looked inside, trying to ignore the horrendous stench, as he noticed two big bright green spots on the far wall two inches apart from each other. He slowly walked further inside the rocks to get a closer look, and saw that the green shiny objects were perfectly round emeralds.

"Mitchell, get away from there!" Stephanie shouted. "The rocks might close up and you'll be stuck in there forever."

"Shh, just hang on a minute. I see something," he told her.

Paul saw what he was looking at, and slowly walked behind him to get a better look for himself. Shauna followed, as Stephanie stayed behind, afraid of everything that could, or would happen.

"Paul, give me your knife. I want to check these things out," Mitchell told him.

Paul reached inside his pocket for his little keychain knife. He opened it up and handed it to Mitchell.

Mitchell slowly walked up against the wall, and looked up at the two emeralds imbedded into the boulder. He admired the stones for a moment and touched one with his fingers. He carefully took the knife and easily pried one of them out. He held the shiny stone in his hand and noticed it was about three inches round, and weighed about two pounds.

Paul examined the wall and saw an out line of a tall humanlike being, carved into the stone that wore a shroud, and had long boney fingers. "This thing looks like some sort of a devil of some sort Mitch, feel this carving."

Mitchell felt the carving around the stone and didn't really care about it as much as he cared about the stones. Mitchell took the knife and pried on the other stone as it easily fell into his hand. The earth suddenly started shaking under them, and smoke began to fill the area as the rocks began to close in. Paul, Shauna, and Mitchell dashed out of the entrance as fast as they could just before the rocks closed in on them.

Mitchell held the stones in his hand, and smiled from ear to ear showing off his findings. He thought of all the money he was going to get for cashing them in, and started to laugh with greed in his eyes.

"I don't think you should have taken those rocks. They must have meant something. There's a reason why they're in there," Stephanie said worried about something horrible was going to happen later on.

"What do you know Steph, and besides, who else knows we took them? No one" he told her and put the stones in his back pack.

"Paul, I think Stephanie is right. Maybe Mitchell should put them back," Shauna agreed.

Paul remembered his mother telling him the story about the green eyes years ago, and began to wonder if they were really the devil's eyes. He began to wonder if the stories his mother told him were real, or if he was just being superstitious so he decided to agree with the girls and put the stones back.

"Mitchell, I think we should reopen the rocks, and put the emeralds back," he said.

"No way!" Mitchell shouted with greed in his eyes. "Do you know how much money we're gonna have?"

"Mitchell, put the rocks back. Screw the money." Paul demanded.

Mitchell stared into his eyes refusing to give in. He looked at the girls staring at him, and shrugged it off. "No, I'm not putting them back." He told them and swung his backpack across his shoulder. He walked up the mountain, and looked back at them wondering if they were going to follow.

Paul started up the mountain behind him as the girls followed. Stephanie looked down at the barb wire fence that Mitchell tripped over, and glanced down at the rocks before she went over and picked up her backpack. When she strapped on her backpack and adjusted the weight on her shoulders, she looked up and saw an old sign nailed to a tree. She walked over and rubbed her hand on the sign. 'Danger Stay away from this area.' she read to herself. She looked around and saw two more danger signs nailed to a tree. "Hey you guys!" she shouted. "There are signs around here that says 'danger' what do you suppose they're there for?" she asked.

"Stephanie come on, you're falling behind!" Shauna shouted.

Stephanie trotted to catch up forgetting about the signs, and put her arm around Shauna. She affectionately gave her a small kiss on the cheek, and walked a few steps ahead of her.

They walked for hours up the mountain, and settled on a place a few minutes walk from the so called summit everyone talked about. They setup camp for the night, and decided to head down the mountain on the other side the following morning.

Mitchell pulled the emeralds out of his backpack, and admired the beautiful green color. He held them up in the air, and let the setting sun shine against the stones. Suddenly Mitchell felt a strong cold draft on the back of his neck. He looked around with curiosity, and quickly slid the stones in his backpack.

Paul and Shauna came back with some firewood, and dropped them down close to Mitchell's feet.

"We got the firewood Mitchell, so you can start the fire," Shauna told him.

"Fine, whatever!" he shouted with an attitude and stood up grabbing some wood.

Paul ignored his comment, and pulled his tent out of his backpack.

Shauna pulled hers and Stephanie's tent out, and started to set it up. Suddenly they all stood there in silence when a long, loud, and deep yell echoed up the mountain. Stephanie swallowed in total fear and looked over at Shauna. Paul tried hard not to show his emotions, as Mitchell chuckled a bit and brushed it off.

"Well, someone's pissed," he said and lit a match to light the fire.

"It's probably the man you stole the emeralds from," Stephanie said and pulled against the tent for Shauna to slide the rod through.

"No, I don't think anybody owns them, Stephanie. Remember they were inside a pair of rocks," Mitchell sneered.

"We should have put them back." Shauna spoke up.

"We should have put them back." Mitchell mocked her. "Forget it. We're not going back down to put them back, and besides, we're going down the other side of the mountain tomorrow. So just forget it."

"Mitchell," Paul spoke with ease. "When we get back to civilization, I don't want to see you for a little while. You're just too much of an asshole lately. I can't take it anymore. I'm sorry Stephanie, but I think you can do better than this loser." He walked over and stuck his hand out in front of Mitchell. "Give me my knife back," he demanded.

Mitchell reached in his pocket without a word, and handed him his knife. He threw another log in the fire, and thought the same about Paul not seeing him for a while either. He thought of the money he was going to make when he cashed in the shiny stones, and imagined himself waving the thousands of dollars in Paul's face when he did and seeing his expression.

Paul finished setting up his tent, and reached down for a beer for the first time since they started hiking. He cracked it open, and quickly guzzled some of it down out of frustration.

Shauna reached in and grabbed a beer for herself, and walked over to Paul. She put her arms around him to comfort him. He looked at her and pulled away to be by himself for a while.

Stephanie sat down on the blanket she stretched out on the ground, and put her coat on. She stared at Mitchell for a moment, and remembered Paul's remark he made. She wondered if it was true, if she could do better, or was he just upset at the time he said it. Shauna came over and sat down next to her. She put her arm around her and smiled. She offered Stephanie a swig of her beer. When she refused, she put the cold can on her neck, and laughed out loud. Stephanie smacked her across the arm out of affection and pushed the beer can away. She crossed her arms, and lost her smile when she started to think about her relationship with Mitchell.

She realized she hated her relationship when Paul said those truthful words, and finally decided she needed to get out. She made up her mind. When they get back home, she was going to call it off. She didn't know how, or when, but she knew it was time. She looked over at Shauna with a fake smile. "I want to talk to you about something later okay," she told her quietly and glanced over at Mitchell pulling the emeralds back out, and admiring the stones.

Suddenly the emeralds shined bright, and lit up the camp with a green ambiance. Paul saw the stones glowing bright, and suddenly got a bad feeling about them. He didn't really believe anything about the unknown since he was a practical kind of guy. His mother always read nonfiction stories to him when he was younger. But he loved to watch horror movies, and thought someday with his strange imagination he was going to write a best selling horror novel.

Mitchell was having fun waving around the stones and admiring the shine, when suddenly they all heard another long, deep yell echoing up the mountain.

Shauna and Stephanie cuddled close, and started to think maybe Paul's story was actually true. Paul looked up in the air, and listened closely for anything out of the ordinary. He stood there for a while and watched Mitchell ignoring the deep yell, and still played with the stones. He shook his head with disappointment, and glanced over at his girlfriend. He looked up at the sky taking a swig of his beer, and saw the moon slowly cutting through the clouds.

"This was a real big mistake," he thought to himself. He couldn't wait to get back home, and get away from Mitchell for a while. What he really wanted was to calm down and spend some quality time with his girl Shauna.

"We need to get up early tomorrow," Paul explained. "So we can head down the mountain, and meet up with Shauna's mother to give us a ride back home."

"I think we all know that," Mitchell spat at him, and looked at him from the corner of his eye.

Paul violently threw his beer can against a tree, and glared at him with swords in his eyes. He turned around and sank himself into his tent fisting his hands, and wanting to punch Mitchell for all its worth. He lied down on his sleeping bag and closed his eyes with Mitchell still on his mind. Shauna and Stephanie stood up from the blanket, and walked away from Mitchell. Shauna jumped in the tent with Paul, as Stephanie stood uncomfortably outside with her arms crossed, waiting, and hoping for an invite. Shauna peaked out and grabbed Stephanie's hand, and pulled her in the tent with her.

Mitchell looked over his shoulder and noticed all of them were in the same tent, and knew they didn't want to be around him. He sat there still holding the glowing stones feeling the heat coming off, and twirling them around in his hand. He thought about when it was a good time it will be to just quietly leave the camp, and not look back.

3

Sunday

Early morning, Paul woke up, and still heard that deep yelling echoing up the mountain. He looked over at Shauna and Stephanie still quietly asleep. He crawled out of the tent, and stretched his body. He looked around the camp, and got a feeling something was different. He walked over to Shauna's tent, and peaked inside to see if Mitchell had crawled in. He wasn't. He looked around the camp a little closer, and noticed Mitchell's backpack was missing.

"Mitchell walked out on us," he said to himself. He walked back to his tent and woke up the girls. Shauna was the first one out of the tent still half asleep and putting her shirt when she saw Paul sitting near the burned out fire and walked over.

"Hey," she said sitting down on the blanket.

"Mitchell's gone," Paul said slipping on his boots.

Shauna looked around the camp and noticed his backpack was missing. "He left us? Well then, the hell with him," she told him.

"We can't just let him walk alone on a mountain that he's never been on, especially this mountain."

"I'm sure the asshole can find his way home on his own. He's a big boy. I'm sure he'll be fine."

Stephanie stepped out of the tent not thinking, and wearing only a white lace bra. Paul turned his head and smiled at her. She smiled back and slipped on her shirt and thought well, seen one boob, seen 'em all. She walked over to the blanket tucking in her shirt, and sat down next to her best friend. "Where's Mitchell?" she asked.

"He took off sometime in the middle of the night," Paul answered her.

Stephanie didn't know whether she wanted to cry, or laugh. But she did know one thing. She wanted him out of her life. "Is that a good thing?" she asked somewhat sarcastic.

"Maybe for you it would be, but he's still our friend no matter how you slice it," He told them.

"Maybe he's your friend," Shauna said. "He's definitely not mine. Not anymore."

"Well, we need to go find him. He's probably lost by now."

"Or, he's probably home sitting in front of the stupid T.V. laughing, and knowing we're still out here looking for him," Shauna said being wise.

"I really don't think so Shauna. It's still a good day of walk down the mountain, and besides, do you honestly think he would go down the dark side alone?"

"Yes I do," Stephanie spoke.

"Paul kicked dirt into the fire pit until the smoke stopped. He quickly tore his tent down and stuffed it into his backpack, and looked over and saw the girls still sitting there and drinking what was left of the water.

"Hello," he said annoyed. "Aren't you going to put your tent away, since you never slept in it last night?"

"What do you care? You got what you wanted," Shauna told him.

"What I want is for you and Stephanie get a move on so we can get going."

"Fine," Stephanie said and got up off the blanket, then waited for Shauna to get up so she could fold it. Shauna walked over to the tent and snapped it down, as Paul helped her pack up to get things done more quickly.

They walked up the mountain and hit the peak in know time at all. They stopped and looked around soaking up the cool refreshing air, and the beautiful scenery.

"Look!" Stephanie shouted, and pointed her finger toward an old broken down log cabin.

"Do you think?" Shauna asked looking at Paul knowing what he was thinking about.

"I don't know, but it's worth a try," He told her.

They walked toward the cabin as Stephanie stared down at the edge of the dark forest. She could feel her skin starting to crawl, and scared herself with her frightening imagination. She clamped onto Shauna's arm and looked square into her eyes. Shauna knew she was scared and tried to hold in the laughter.

Paul slowly stepped onto the old porch. The wood creaked and sagged with every step. He looked through the broken door with his hand against the untreated logs, and saw everything covered with dust and dirt from years of build up. Daylight shined through between the logs from the wind finally pushing the dried pressed clay to the floor.

The legs of the old wooden table were covered with thick black mold, both chairs were broken, and the floor had years of tall grass growing up between the cracks. He saw an old black and white picture of a man holding a rifle hanging on the wall. It had pieces of broken glass still inside the wooden frame. He walked over to the picture and stared at the bearded husky man. The man had posed for the camera without a smile, and stood next to the door of his cabin they trespassed upon. He wondered about the rifle he was holding, and shifted his eyes around the cabin hoping for a miracle left behind. He looked back at the picture and noticed a small piece of yellow paper sticking out from the bottom. He slowly pulled out the folded paper and carefully opened it up. He read the name 'Major Samuel Har' on the top, but he couldn't make out the rest of the last name. He read a few more untainted words he could make out, but he barely could read the name 'General Grant' on the bottom.

Shauna walked in and quickly spun her head in all directions looking at everything, seeing if Mitchell or anything there was left behind from him. She somewhat hoped he was here, and to give her some kind of relief that he was still alive. She didn't know why but she just needed to know.

Paul folded the paper back up and carefully put it in his backpack to take home with him for further examination. He had a feeling it was an old letter from the Civil war, but he wasn't totally sure. He walked over to the homemade bed made from a birch tree pressed against the wall, and noticed the old pillow had an indent in the middle like someone had just slept on it. He touched the pillow; it felt hard and stale, and felt the years of dust on his fingers. He carefully lifted the old blanket, and saw the bones of a small dead animal that died trying to get warm.

Stephanie looked inside from the door watching her friends examine the abandoned cabin. She crossed her arms tight feeling her goose bumps and constantly looked down at the edge of the dark forest wondering if their going in there, and are they going to come out alive. Her imagination frightened her as she closed her eyes and tried to blank out her thoughts.

Shauna glanced over at her with a smile, and walked into a spider web spread across the window and up to the beam on the roof. Paul looked out the window and saw just ahead, an old fire pit still holding a big black pot in the middle with smaller ones hanging of the side of the stone wall around the pit. He glanced down at the ground, and saw fresh boot prints in the dirt.

"Mitchell was here," he said. "There are prints from his boots right there in the dirt."

Shauna walked over and looked at the prints. She knew his boot marks made a deep mark, and knew they were his. She sighed with some relief, but still, even though she can't stand the sight of him, she needed more than just a print. Paul walked outside and looked down at the dark forest. He glanced up the mountain wondering which direction Mitchell would have gone, and then saw an old cross sticking out of the ground. He thought of the man in the picture, and walked up to the old cross. He looked at it and read the name 'Hartwell' carved into it. He wondered when the man died, did he live alone, or who even buried him, and when? "So many questions," he thought. Mitchell popped back into his thoughts, and again he wondered which way did he head down through the forest, or if he even did.

"Let's get going," he told them. "I want to get out of here before the sun goes down."

Shauna tightened her backpack, and headed down the mountain behind Paul. Stephanie walked closely behind Shauna an arms length away, just in case.

"When we get into the forest," Shauna spoke. "The sun is going to be down anyway."

"What do you mean?" Stephanie asked.

"What I mean is the forest doesn't have any light in there. That's why it's called the dark forest."

"We're walking all the way into the forest?" Stephanie asked pointing her finger and getting more and more frightened.

"Yes Stephanie," Paul told her and started to chuckle.

Stephanie was getting scared with every step she made. She reached out to touch Shauna for comfort but quickly pulled her hand away.

They stopped in front of the forest and stared into nothing but darkness. They all stood there and remained quiet staring into the forest listening to the sound of silence. No birds were singing, no crickets were chirping, nothing. Each one of them was scared to enter, especially Stephanie. But Paul knew if he didn't go in, the years of dreaming about this place would crumble in his own thoughts. He knew if he didn't get up the nerve, he would always have it in the back of his mind how one step into the forest would have fulfilled his destiny, as well as his dreams.

"Well, there's no use in standing here. Let's go before we don't go," he told them stepping into the forest. He didn't even look back, not once. Shauna followed few steps away, and as for Stephanie, she couldn't get any closer to Shauna without stepping on her heels. Paul pulled the flashlight out of the side his backpack and clicked on the switch. He pointed the flashlight down to the ground and saw the mushy feeling they were stepping on of the thick dead pine needles. They walked into the dark side of the mountain hoping to see the other end of the forest, and daylight.

A half an hour into the deep dark forest, Paul stopped for a moment and put his ears to work. He kept hearing a strange wheezing noise coming just yards away. He shined the light around the forest and tried to pin point where the noise was coming from. Shauna yanked the flashlight out of her backpack, and quickly shined it through the trees looking for the noise. She saw something shiny reflecting, as she slowly walked toward where it was coming from. Stephanie gripped her backpack tight, as Paul walked behind still listening for the weird sound. Suddenly, Stephanie screamed as loud as she could and pointed her finger up to the trees. Shauna quickly shined her light up.

"There!" Stephanie shouted. "There! It's Mitchell!" Paul shined his light up and saw his friend hanging from a rope wrapped around his neck. He was barely moving and almost ten feet up. His face was red, and his eyes were starting to turn bloodshot. His wrists were wrapped inside the rope as he tried pushing the rope away from his neck with what strength he had left. He was alive but starting giving up on life.

"Jesus H. Christ Paul, he's choking to death!" Shauna screamed in frantic.

Paul followed the rope down to where it tied onto a branch, and ran over to cut it down. He pulled the knife out of his pocket, jumped up and pulled down on the branch, and sawed against the rope until Mitchell fall hard to the ground. Stephanie and Shauna ran over to him as he took one big gasping breath of relief.

Stephanie carefully loosened the noose and took it off his neck, and then threw it on the ground.

"What the hell are these ropes for anyway?" she asked.

"They're traps the Indians made for hunting," Paul explained. "But the Indian's haven't been on this mountain for a hundred years."

"Then who put them up?" Shauna asked.

"I don't know," Paul said thinking of Mr. Hartwell lying dead in the ground. He grabbed the rope and wondered if Mr. Hartwell hung them before he died, or if someone else was living alone on the mountain like he did.

Shauna shined the light on Mitchell and saw his neck, and both of his wrists were rope burned and bleeding. Mitchell took another deep breath and let out a huge choking cough. He lied on his stomach and rested his head on the mushy pine needles breathing heavy, coughing, and tearing uncontrollably.

Stephanie looked down at Mitchell, and for the first time, she felt no remorse and unsympathetic. In some wishful sense, she wished they had found him just hanging there swinging lifeless in the breeze. She wished he was dead.

She looked over at Shauna sitting there, waiting for him to calm down as Paul patted his back.

"I think you almost did yourself in that time Mitchell," Paul said with a chuckle and sat down next to Shauna.

"I've been hanging there since…. Christ I don't know how long it's been." Mitchell rolled over on to his back, and looked at Paul holding the light on him.

"I knew everyone was mad at me, so I left. I thought I could walk home and just forget about everything." He looked over at Stephanie, as Stephanie quickly turned her head in another direction. He knew she didn't want any part of him, and has to come to realize it was his fault that their relationship crumbled.

Paul stood up, and held his hand out to help Mitchell on his feet. Mitchell rolled over and slowly stood up on his own. He put his hand on his neck and felt the blood on his fingers. Shauna shined the light on him and noticed the collar of his shirt was soaked with blood. Mitchell snapped the backpack off him letting it fall to the ground, and rubbed his wrists feeling the intense pain the rope had left. He pulled in a long deep breath, and exhaled slowly.

"Do you think you can walk with us?" Paul asked.

Mitchell picked up his backpack, and clipped it back on. He still felt the burning across his neck and wrists, but the only thing he thought about was going home and being alone for a while.

Stephanie walked by him without saying a word and grabbed Shauna's backpack.

Paul lead the way back down the mountain, constantly looking back to make sure his friends were okay, and being on the look out for more of those hanging rope traps.

For the next three hours an occasional word was spoken. Everyone was tired, but Paul was determined to get his friends out of the forest before night fall, or did it already? He looked up to the sky, but the branches were too thick to see anything but sheer darkness. Shauna's flashlight was dimming, and Stephanie still held on to her backpack tight. Suddenly Paul stopped. He looked around and saw a lot more ropes hanging down from the trees. He slowly walked around the traps, every once in a while cutting down the ones he could reach.

Mitchell lightly touched his neck in remembrance looking at the hanging ropes. Paul stopped again, feeling his foot sink in something softer than the mushy needles. He looked down shining the light on his foot. He saw a dead half eaten wolf with a rope around its neck. His foot was resting on its maggot infested stomach. The stench was horrendous, and he saw more bugs worming around on the decaying animal. Stephanie covered her mouth and tried not to scream as Shauna looked on hiding her own fear. Paul slowly took his foot off and backed two steps away scraping it on the needles. They all stared at the dead wolf for a moment and wondered. "What animal eats wolves?" Paul scrambled the animals through his head, bears, birds, fox, or more wolves. "Wolves," he thought. "Shit, that's all we need, is to tangle with wolves." he kept his thoughts to himself, so he wouldn't get his friends in a panic.

Right then, they all stopped in their tracks when they heard the quiet sound of a growl coming from within the deep dark forest. Shauna smacked her flashlight hoping the light would brighten up. Paul slowly shined his light in all directions, as Stephanie saw the reflection of the wolf's eyes glowing.

"Paul," Stephanie said quietly. "Give me the flashlight for a minute." Paul moved the flashlight around swiftly, and didn't see anything. He handed her the flashlight as she shined it right on the wolf. The wolf stood there watching them panting as though he's been waiting for his food.

Stephanie saw the wolf swiftly moving its head back and forth, and knew there were others near by. She remembered doing a study on wolves in science class when she was in the tenth grade. She knew wolves didn't stray alone unless they were hurt, at least she didn't think so.

They all stood there, watching the wolf still moving his head back and forth, and his legs weren't moving from the spot he was in. Stephanie remembered her teacher saying if you're ever in a bind, don't move fast, and don't ever take your eyes off the wolf. She kept the flashlight on the animal and pushed against Shauna's backpack for her to move forward. Paul started to walk down the mountain feeling his way keeping his hands out in front of him for any more rope traps. Mitchell stayed behind watching the wolf in the light. Suddenly Paul stopped, as Shauna bounced off his backpack. Stephanie mistakenly turned the flashlight toward Paul and quickly turned it back to the wolf. The wolf was gone. She started to panic when she couldn't find the wolf anywhere. Shauna smacked her flashlight one last time when finally the light brightened up. She swiftly moved her flashlight around looking for the wolf. She started to get frightened for everyone's life, especially her own.

Suddenly Paul heard a deep growl directly ahead of him. Shauna slowly flashed her light and shined it on the wolf. The wolf took a couple steps closer to them as Paul and Shauna backed away. Mitchell looked behind him and saw more shadows moving within the darkness. He quickly grabbed the flashlight from Stephanie's hand and shined it on a wolf running past them.

"Paul, we're surrounded," Mitchell said and saw another wolf running by closer to them.

"I see that Mitchell. Got any ideas?" he swallowed hard.

"Not yet."

"Fire," Stephanie spoke up. "They don't like fire."

"Great," I'll start a fire, and…."

A wolf howled loud echoing the forest. They all stood there in silence fearing for their lives. Shauna was starting to silently cry as Stephanie bent down to pick up a dry branch she saw near her foot. She dug her finger nail into her clothing ripping a large piece off the bottom of her shirt, and tightly wrapped it around the stick. "Paul, give me your lighter," she told him.

"Steph, I don't have a lighter," he replied.

"Paul, give me your lighter, or I'll rip it out of your pocket," she demanded. Shauna looked at Paul, and stuck her hand down his pocket. She pulled out the lighter, and handed it to Stephanie. She stared into his eyes and knew something was being kept a secret from her. She was determined to find out later on when, or if they get home. Stephanie lit the stick on fire, and suddenly saw all of the wolves in a circle with them in the middle.

"Oh shit," Paul said looking at Mitchell.

Mitchell looked over at Paul and noticed he was standing next to a dead man hanging from the trees. He was already half eaten. His clothes were torn to shreds. His left leg was ripped from his body, and his right hand was bitten off at the wrist. Paul turned around and saw the dead man. He froze for a moment and stared at the half eaten corpse. Some of the man's side was bitten off; his blood had dried against his skin, and drooled down to the pine needle covered ground.

Paul had a strong feeling the man hadn't been there long, and he didn't recognize his face. Paul quickly thought of an idea, and knew the only way to do it was to have all of his friends work together, and cut the dead man off the tree and run as fast as they could. The wolves were getting anxious, and waiting for the flame to burn out. Shauna looked over at Paul and saw the dead man hanging. She screamed as loud as she could, startling the wolves as they ferociously started barking, growling, and snapping their jaws. Paul grabbed the flame out of Stephanie's hand and swung it around to back the wolves away. He looked to where the rope trap was tied to, and slowly walked toward the branch. Mitchell knew what Paul was doing and quietly nudged Shauna and Stephanie to follow him. Paul dug the knife out of his pocket, and cut the dead man down off the tree. The wolves quickly jumped at the dead man ripping the decaying meat, and his bones away. They could hear the wolves fighting amongst each other of which one got the biggest piece of food.

"Run," Paul said quietly. "Now!" he screamed and grabbed Shauna's hand. Mitchell grabbed Stephanie's hand and took off behind Paul as fast as he could and pulling her along, and didn't let go.

A couple wolves watched them running, but stayed with the pack for the bloody feast. Stephanie started to cry with fear and heard Shauna crying also. Paul held the flame in front of him, and dodged anything and everything in the way. They heard the wolves still growling and fighting amongst each other feasting on what the wolves would call, 'a kill'. No one looked back. No one wanted to. They ran, and they kept running until Shauna pulled her hand away from Paul.

Paul ran back, and grabbed her again. He yanked on her hand, but she refused to run. Mitchell let go of Stephanie's hand and saw a good sign off in the distance catching his breath. It was daylight. Mitchell started to smile with relief, and knew they've made it out of the dark forest. His neck was burning worse than before from running, and from the sweat running down from his hair.

"Shauna," Paul spoke. "We need to get the hell out of here. The wolves, maybe they'll…"

"The wolves are gone," She interrupted. "They're eating that dead man you cut down. I'm sure there not going to care about where we are anymore."

Paul looked around, and put his hands down on his knees. He saw the clearing Mitchell was walking down to, looked at the burned out stick, and stuck it deep into the soft ground. He looked over at Stephanie. Her shirt was ruined, and it revealed the bottom of her lace bra. She didn't care, she didn't want to care, she wanted to go home, and it was written all over her face. Paul walked down toward the clearing and looked back hoping the girls were following. Mitchell walked out of the dark forest and looked up at the sky with a smile, and then slid down the grass to the road. He sat down on the wet ground, unsnapped his backpack from his shoulders, and took a deep breath. He felt Paul's hand on his shoulder as he sat down next to him. The girls were standing behind Paul, still, both were catching there breath from running.

"Is this where we're supposed to be picked up?" Paul asked.

"I have no idea," Shauna said. "But I'll tell you one thing. I'm never going to hike this friggin mountain again."

"Here, here," Stephanie agreed.

Mitchell stood up and looked down both ways of the road. He noticed the air was moist, and the sky was cloudy. Then after a few minutes he realized they were only half way down the mountain. He looked back at his friends and shook his head. "I'm gonna catch a ride from the next car that comes down the road," Mitchell said. "I've had enough of this shit."

"Can I come with you?" Stephanie asked and looked at Shauna.

"Me too?" Shauna asked.

Paul looked at Shauna, and knew that she too has had enough, and so wanted to go home. He gave in and walked out to the road, and stood next to Mitchell with his thumb out.

Mitchell started to wave his arms high in the air hoping the huge tractor trailer truck he saw would stop and pick them up. Then, Mitchell smiled with relief when he heard the air brakes, and the truck started to slow down. He ran over and picked up his backpack and jumped into the truck. He put his hand out for Stephanie, and helped her into the truck. Shauna jumped in, and then Paul jumped in and slammed the passenger door. He introduced himself and his friends to the long-haired female truck driver who felt a little crammed in and somewhat thought maybe she had made a mistake picking them all up. She told him she was heading to Glencliff to drop off supplies at the hardware store. Paul smiled a bit with relief and looked at his friends, and looked down at the clock on the radio. "It's 4:15," he said out loud. "Your mother isn't supposed to pick us up until six. We'll make it home way before then." Shauna smiled at the driver, and put her hand on Paul's shoulder.

"Thank you," she said to the driver. "Thank you for picking us up. We live in Glencliff, and it would be great if you could drop us off at the convenience store right on Main Street."

"Sure, the driver said. "It's not a problem at all. Just return the favor someday if you ever see me broken down on the side of the road." She smiled at Paul and down shifted the truck.

4

Paul woke up from his usual nap late Thursday afternoon thinking of another story that's been stuck in his head since they came off the mountain. It was about the old man he sometimes sees that lives next door. He smiled a bit, and looked out the window at the old man's front porch where he liked to sit peacefully like every retired man does, and whittle a small piece of wood hoping to carve out that special gift to give to their grandson.

He glanced over at his computer and thought about when it was the right time to sit down and start writing the story, before his thoughts vanish like the years to come, or was there time? That thought scared him the most.

He hadn't seen Mitchell or Stephanie since they came off the mountain. Shauna only stopped by once since they argued about him admitting the fact he started smoking again. He promised Shauna he would quit, but the cravings were too much for him, and secretly he had never really stopped. He jumped off his bed and slumped down the staircase to the kitchen where his mother was baking pies for the weekend church bake off sale. He could smell the blueberries and the apples, and started to get hungry. He opened the swinging door and saw Shauna with an apron on full of flour, and a smile.

"What's up Smokey," Shauna said sarcastically.

"Ha, ha very funny," he said back to her.

"Smokey?" his mother questioned. "Paul, do you smoke?" she asked looking at him with her burning blue eyes, and waited for his honest answer. Paul knew he was stuck in a spot where if he lied to her, he was doomed forever in going to church. He didn't think being a church-goer was his cup of tea.

"Yes Mom, I smoke cigarettes," he told her disappointingly. "But I have only a couple a day, and they're lights."

His mother put the knife down after she cut the edge off the pie. She looked at him, and swung her blonde hair away from her disappointed face. She walked over to him and stared into his eyes. Shauna saw Shauna smirking behind her with that "you're in trouble" look on her face, and crossed her arms leaning against the table. Shauna knew he should have never lied to Shauna, and now he's gonna regret ever even knowing her.

"Shauna," his mother spoke with a low tone of voice. "You have ten days to decide whether your going to smoke, or find another place to live. Nobody in this house smokes cancer sticks, and nobody will. You have ten days to decide." She picked the knife up, and started cutting the edge off the pie. Shauna still stared at him with her eyebrows crooked. She imitated smoking from her fingers, until Shauna's mother looked up and caught her. Shauna rolled his eyes and left the room, the same time Shauna looked over at his mother grinning, who was also smiling from ear to ear. Shauna had planned the whole thing, and included his mother to help him stop. She knew the only way to get him to listen was to get his mother involved. It worked, and she knew it worked. Waiting the ten days was a piece of cake, she knew Shauna's mother played a good role as a mom, and never would actually kick Shauna out of the house. Since she became a single mom at the early age of barely sixteen, it quickly taught her the ropes of being independent, and teaching her son Shauna never lie to his own mother.

"Think he'll quit this time?" Shauna asked.

Shauna's mother stopped what she was doing, and looked at Shauna still smiling. "He'll quit," she said.

Shauna felt relieved after she said that, and wanted to go over and give her a hug. But she felt if she did, she would over step her boundaries since being a member of the family didn't exist, not just yet anyway.

Paul started to walk up the stairs back to his room secretly flipping the middle finger to Shauna for ratting him out when he noticed the paper on the corner table where everyone drops their keys. He pulled it out from under the People magazine and skipped to the classifications. He wanted to buy a used motorcycle, and wanted to ride out west on the bike when he travels to college. His mother kept telling him that a motorcycle is not a way to travel, especially when you have a lot of things to carry. He dropped the paper back down and unconsciously read the bottom headlines of an article just under a small picture of a man. He walked three steps up the stairs, stopped and turned around and read it again. "Man still missing after one month" He read some more of the article, and looked at the black and white picture again. He noticed the man in the picture looked just like the same man they saw hanging from the tree. He took the paper and walked back into the kitchen.

"Look at this guy in the picture Shauna," he told her and handed her the paper.

Shauna looked at the picture wondering who he was, and then suddenly she remembered where she saw him. She put her hand over her mouth, and looked at his mother. Paul's mother leaned over and looked at the picture. She wondered who the man was and what was going on.

"Do you know this man?" she asked, and wiped her hands on her apron.

"Not exactly," Paul said. "We saw him up in the dark forest."

"Well, if you saw him at the forest, then why don't you call the police and tell them you saw the man."

"Mom, I don't think they'll ever find him."

"Why, you said you saw him, right?"

"Yes we did see him. But he was already dead when we found him."

"More like half eaten if you ask me," Shauna said putting her two cents in.

His mother untied her apron and sat down at the table. She gestured both of them to sit down and tell her the whole story. "Let's hear it," She told them demandingly.

"Mom it's not what you think."

"Then I suggest you tell me what I should think."

"We stopped at the top of the mountain, when we had a fall out with Mitchell. He was being a real jerk."

"Yeah, all he cared about was those damn green emeralds we found," Shauna threw in.

Just then Paul's mother looked at them with a frightening look on her face. She stared at Shauna with fear. Her hands started to shake, and she slowly stood up from the table. She quickly ran to the phone and dialed the police non-emergency phone number. Paul and Shauna looked at her and wondered why she hurried to the phone, and who she was calling.

"Bill Parsons please," she told the dispatcher.

"Mom!" Paul shouted nervously. "Why are you calling the chief of police? We didn't kill the guy. He was already dead."

"Bill, this is Jessica Michaels. Paul's... I'm fine, but we have a really big problem. The stones, yes, the emeralds, they're out of the rocks again."

Paul and Shauna listened to her talking to the chief. Paul realized she didn't even care about the missing man they were trying to tell her. All she cared about was the green emeralds Mitchell found. "Please, we need to get them back quickly. I don't know if it's too late. Mitchell Straw has them as far as I know, okay, bye... okay... hurry." She nervously hung up the phone and leaned against the wall.

"Mom, what the hell is going on? Why did you call the police? Why did you call the chief?" he asked.

"Mitchell has the emeralds?" His mother asked.

"Yes, he found them in some place in the mountain that had two huge rocks leaning against each other."

"How did you open up the rocks up?"

32.

"Why, what's the big deal?"

"Answer me Paul. How did you open the rocks?"

"I read some strange words on a rock we found that was covered with dirt, why?"

"The rocks opened up on their own. You didn't force the rocks open?"

"No, the rocks just opened up, and we saw the emeralds inside. That's when Mitchell pried the stones out of the wall with my pocket knife."

"Jess," Shauna said softly. "What's wrong? What did we do?" she asked getting very scared they did something they shouldn't have.

"Paul, Shauna, You don't know what you just did. You don't understand."

"Mom, then tell us what we did so friggin bad," Paul said as he himself was getting scared.

"You woke up an evil curse, and now people will die if we don't get those stones back where they belong."

Shauna heard the word curse, and her eyes started to fill up with tears. She thought about her friends, and then put her hand on Paul's arm.

"So, we'll just go and get the stones from Mitchell, and go put them back. That's simple enough." Paul told her.

"No, it's not that easy. Paul you don't know what you have done. I do."

"Mom, what do you mean, you do?"

"Remember the stories I told you when you were younger?"

"Yeah,"

"It's all true. I was there, and I lost three of my best friends back then because of the curse."

"What happened?" Shauna asked.

Paul's mother looked into their eyes, and remembered her friends for a brief moment.

"The Phantom," she whispered picturing the horrible Phantom in her memory just like it was yesterday.

"Explain to us about the Phantom," Shauna told her.

She walked over and sat down at the kitchen table. She put her elbow on the table, and remembered everything what happened to her 25 years ago. She remembered seeing the Phantom so close up she could touch him, and then quickly felt a chill go up her spine when she thought of the Phantom's pointed boney fingers.

"I remember it so clear. The Phantom was the most terrifying thing I've ever seen. Paul and Shauna sat down, and listened to her start telling them the story about the Dark Mountain Phantom.

"We were your age back then. You were just a baby Paul. We got a bunch of friends together to go up the mountain. Like you, we heard about the legend of Dark Mountain from an old man who always sat on the park bench, and wore a pair of black sunglasses and walked with a cane. He was blind, but nobody knew that at the time. Every time we would go into town, we always saw the old man sitting in front of the candy store. He would smile, and talk to us like he could see us. He told us one day we would make the same mistake he did, and regret it for the rest of our lives…. He was right." She shook her head wiped the tears from her eyes, and remembered the old man sitting in front of the candy store.

"So, what happened?" Shauna said softly.

"The old man told us one day about some green emeralds, and where they were. But he never said, don't go up the mountain and get them. We never saw him again after that day. One day on a whim, we got everyone together including chief William Parsons, and went up the mountain to find the stones. There were six of us. We ran up the mountain laughing and carrying on like a bunch of wild kids like it was the last day of school, and searched the mountain for the twin rocks as the old man had called them. We found the rocks by mistake, when Lou accidentally tripped and fell down the mountain and smacked his head against the rocks giving him self a minor concussion.

"Billy was the first to slide down to see if he was okay, when he noticed the rocks were slightly opened. The rest of us got together and pulled against them, and I was the one who rolled another rock between them to hold the rocks open wide enough to slide through. Lou saw the emeralds on the back wall, and went in and got them. We didn't know it at the time, but the emeralds were glowing in the bag Lou put them in. Suddenly the rocks started to fill up with smoke, and they closed up smashing the smaller rock into little pieces. We ran down the mountain as fast as we could, talking about how much money we were going to get for them, and what we were going to buy."

"Mitchell did the same thing," Paul interrupted.

"Anyways, on the way down we heard the sound of an eerie deep loud yelling, like someone was hurt or stuck in a deep hole. The noise we heard was that of the Dark Mountain Phantom."

Paul and Shauna looked at each other, and thought about the yelling they heard on the top of the mountain.

"A couple days later, some of us heard Billy's father talking to someone about Lou. His parents found him in his room tucked in a corner. They said his eyes were dug out of his sockets, and he was lying down in a fetal position with a broken neck. The next day they found my best friend Michelle. They said her skin was white as a ghost. Her eyes were also missing, and she was also lying in a fetal position dead. My friend Lisa was found near Woodland Bridge. She was face down in the water, her neck was broken, and her eyes were also missing. They said the Phantom was looking for his eyes--- which--- were the emerald stones?"

Shauna's stomach turned, and her head started to spin. She thought about the stones and realized her friends including herself were about to get killed, and leaned her head against Paul's arm.

"The bad thing about it is. The only ones, who can see the Dark Mountain Phantom, are the ones who saw the rocks split open and revealed the emeralds."

"How did the stone's get back into the rocks?" Paul asked.

His mother looked at the floor, and remembered the time when she was face to face with the evil Phantom.

"Billy saved my life. He found the stones in Lou's bedroom, and tossed them to me. I picked up the stones and handed them to the Phantom. The Phantom carefully took them from me dragging his pointy finger across the palm of my hand, and placed them in his eyes with somewhat of a smile. After that it was weird, he just disappeared right in front of us. But I'll never forget those pointed boney fingers. That's how Lou's, Michelle's, and Lisa's eyes were removed from their sockets. I've never been so scared in all my life."

Silence fell over the room as Paul's mother finished telling them the story of her frightening experience. Suddenly everyone jumped when there was a loud knock at the door; Paul's mother knew it was her high school friend the police chief. Paul jumped up and walked out to the living room to open the front door. Chief Parsons walked in with three other police officers, and called out his mother's name. Paul's mother came out from the kitchen and for the first time since they were kids, she reached out and gave him a big hug and held him tight. She let go and looked at him up and down with admiration. She thought how he's gotten better with age. No more long blonde hair, and that awful scraggily beard she hated was finally gone. Instead he was a handsome man with broad shoulders, blue eyes, and his hair was a half an inch off his head. She admired his strength, his looks, his personality, and his leadership as a police officer. Most of all, she secretly wished she married him, instead of getting pregnant in the eleventh grade, and then getting dumped by her high school boyfriend, who, the last she heard was spending more than enough time in the Concord House of Correction for two counts of vehicular homicide.

She remembered reading that in the newspaper sometime ago. He was speeding over a blind hill in his big Chevy truck, and slammed into a couple of kids riding double on a moped killing them both on impact. The newspaper also said he sat on the side of the road and waited for the police to arrive, and when they did. He told the police the kids were instant road pizza. When the investigation was final, he got four plus years for each kid.

"Jess, we need to know everything," The chief said and looked into her blue eyes.

"Billy, I want you to save my son and his friends. I need you more than ever now."

"Jess, the only thing I can say is. I can do the best I can. Without seeing the Phantom, it's like catching someone's imagination."

"Let's sit down and have them tell us everything that they did. Then, we can take it from there."

5

Mitchell dozed off on his bed in front of the television. He started to dream he was walking through the dark forest. He saw the light of his flashlight bouncing off every tree, and felt the mushy pine needles with every step. The rope traps that hung from the trees scared him the most as his body twitched in his sleep, and unconsciously he put his hand on his neck feeling the burn marks. He pictured himself hanging as the rope squeezed his neck tighter and tighter while he gasped for air. He saw the rope burns on his neck and wrists. He looked down at his hands and noticed they were covered in blood, and looked up and saw the eyes of the wolf reflecting in the light. His body twitched again when he felt himself running as fast as he could through the forest. Suddenly he saw a strange man off in the distance and stopped. He shined the flashlight through the trees, and saw he was a tall man wearing a dark shroud that covered his body and face. He looked at the man as he walked closer, curious to see who he was. The man slowly uncovered his face, as he saw the emeralds shine bight in the man's eyes. Mitchell's body twitched again as he saw the deep lines up and down his face oozing with blood. His nose was long, and bent downward like a witch. His mouth was open and filled with smoke floating around like a fast moving cloud.

"Mitchell." He heard his name echoing. He looked at the man but he was unsure if it was him saying his name. "Mitchell." He heard his name again through the trees. He saw the man coming closer holding his long boney fingers out.

"Mitchell!" He felt his shoulder moving rapidly. "Mitchell!" He opened his eyes and saw his mother standing over him shouting his name.

"What," He said yawning, and stretched his arms over his head.

"I found this letter in the trash. Will you kindly tell me why you didn't get accepted to NYU?" she asked him demandingly.

Mitchell sat up and thought of the weird dream he just had, and wondered what it all meant. He felt the burn marks on his neck, and looked at the marks on his wrists.

"I'm waiting," his mother said harsh.

"I didn't get accepted, because my grades suck. Besides, they said they already have enough basketball players anyway. I've been thinking about taking some time off, and explore some of my options."

"The only thing you're going to explore is the end of my foot. You either go to college, or find a good paying job!" She ordered and stormed out of his room, and slammed the door.

Mitchell slid himself on the bed, and stretched again brushing off her 1950's attitude. He looked down at the backpack, and remembered the stones he left in the side pocket. He walked out of his room and went down the stairs to grab something to eat. There was a knock on the door as he got to the bottom. He walked over and opened the door. "Steph!" he said surprisingly. "What's going on?"

"Nothing, can I come in?" she stepped in before he could answer and shut the door.

Mitchell looked at her. He sensed something was wrong. He knew exactly why she came over, but he decided to play dumb anyway.

"Why haven't you called me?" she asked. "Not that I give a shit anymore, but why haven't you called?"

Mitchell stuck his hands in his pockets, and felt the seam of his pants dig against the burn marks. He quickly pulled them out, and crossed his arms.

"I've been busy," he said.

"Doing what, Sleeping?"

"No," he lied to her, and again he thought of the weird dream he just had.

"Mitchell, we need to talk about us," she said and walked into the living room. She plumped herself down, and crossed her arms and legs.

Mitchell stood there for a minute, glanced into the kitchen looking for his aging mother. He slowly walked in the living room, and sat in his father's recliner across from her. He snapped the foot rest out, and looked at her with his cold uncaring eyes.

Stephanie took a deep breath and thought of all the rehearsing she had done at home in front of the mirror. She wanted out of the relationship. She wanted out now, but she was too scared he might go crazy and do something, or even hurt her some how.

"Steph," he said softly. "I think that uh, we should start thinking about seeing other people," he said beating her to the punch.

Stephanie's eyes widened. She couldn't believe what she just heard. She couldn't believe he was thinking of the same thing. She took a deep breath and smiled as she exhaled. "What a load off my mind," she thought.

"You were thinking about breaking up too?" She asked.

"Well," he pulled a lie out of his ass. "I'm going to NYU in the fall, and you're going to UNH. We're going to be too far away from each other to have a relationship."

Stephanie sat there and listened to every word he said. She wanted to jump for joy, and most of all, she wanted to thank him for not getting upset. She stood up from the couch and walked over to him with her hand out. She was still nervous and slightly scared, but the thought of being free from his tight hold was enough to let her self feel good inside.

He shook her hand with a smile, quickly kicked in the foot rest, and stood up. He towered over her and smiled strangely when he looked deep into her eyes. She started to get frightened, and stepped back from him.

"You need to go now. I think are relationship has been over for quite some time. But we had fun on our little trip up the mountains didn't we?" Mitchell asked, and walked over to the door.

"Yeah, I guess so, considering we were arguing most of the time," she replied and walked toward the door behind him. She hoped and prayed he was going to just let her leave without a fight, and then surprisingly she watched him slowly open the door. She stepped out onto the concrete steps, turned around and looked at him one more time.

"Are we still going to be friends" she asked nervously and thought of all the brutal things Mitchell would want to do to her, or even kill her.

Mitchell evilly stared into her eyes. He wanted to scream bloody blue murder. He wanted to yell at her as loud as he could, and tell her just where she can go. He felt enraged with anger as his eyes starting to fill up with tears. He nodded his head at her with a fake, but yet, a revengeful smile.

She nervously turned around and walked down the sidewalk waiting for that gunshot to the back. He watched her for a moment, glaring at her, steaming inside, and still, he wanted to scream. Suddenly, the whole neighborhood echoed from Mitchell slamming the front door as hard as he could.

She quickly ran to her car scared as scared as she could be, and drove away as fast as she could.

She thought about calling her best friend Shauna, and telling her everything what just happened. But she knew it wasn't over yet.

"Something is wrong. Something isn't right," she thought. "Mitchell just doesn't give up this easy." She became more and more frightened as she kept thinking of Mitchell slamming that door. She started to think of the future, and what evil nightmare it will bring. She also wondered if she'll even see the sun come up the next day. Stephanie started to shake in panic as her foot stepped harder on the accelerator when the tires skidded around the corner heading toward Woodland Bridge. She thought of Mitchell's obsessive ness that could get her killed. She knew she was his dream girl, and she knew she meant everything to him. She wanted to cry, but the first thing she wanted to do was go hide and never come out. She reached in her bag, pulled out her cell phone and dialed Shauna's cell number, and hit send. She glanced back up at the road and saw a big German Shepard dog standing in the middle of the road. She quickly swerved the car losing control. She dropped her cell phone on the floor, quickly grabbed the steering wheel with both hands, and crashed through the guard rail. Her car slid and bounced down the embankment. Shauna's phone started to ring in her bag as she was sitting in the living room with Paul and the police. She ran into the kitchen, turned on her phone and put it to her ear.

"Hello," she said and heard the sound of a woman screaming. Stephanie pressed her foot on the brake as hard as she could as her car still slid down the hill, and saw a big tree directly in front of her. She turned the steering wheel and screamed louder as the car kept sliding right for the tree. She screamed louder in panic as the front of her car slammed into the tree.

"Hello, Steph is that you? Are you okay?" Shauna got worried when she heard the screaming and Stephanie didn't answer. She kept the line open hoping Stephanie would say something on the phone. "Stephanie, are you there. Say something!" she shouted.

Paul hurried into the kitchen when he heard her shouting. "What's the matter?" He asked worried. "I don't know. I heard Stephanie screaming, and then there was absolute silence. But her phone is still on," he asked.

Paul's mother and the chief came into the kitchen the same time the chief's radio went on. He turned up his radio as the dispatcher was announcing there's been an accident on Main Street at the Woodland Bridge. The chief radioed back and told the dispatcher he was en-route. The chief and the other police officers trotted out the door to their cruisers and took off with the lights flashing, and sirens blaring.

"I'm going to find out if it is Stephanie in that accident," Shauna told them. She grabbed her bag and took off out the door still holding the phone to her ear.

"Wait!" Paul shouted. "I'm going with you!" Shauna started the car and put it in gear when Paul shut the passenger door.

She drove down the road worried and hoped it wasn't Stephanie. She still listened for any noise, when she started to hear the siren's on Stephanie's phone getting louder. She knew then it was Stephanie, and she started to think of the worst. Paul pulled the phone from her ear, and listened in. He faintly heard the sounds of people in the background, and then he heard a woman's voice moaning softly.

"She's alive. I can hear her," He said.

"Are you sure it's her?" Shauna asked.

Paul looked at her and paused for a moment. "No, I'm not sure," he said.

Shauna screeched the tires turning the corner and saw the police, the ambulance, and fire trucks blocking the road. She stopped the car, got out leaving her car door wide open, and ran up to the scene. She looked down the embankment, and saw Stephanie's car in a pile of rubble smashed against the tree just a few feet from the rivers edge.

Paul looked down at the road and saw the skid marks she made in the grass all the way down the hill. He wondered how fast she was driving to smash through a steel barrier. Suddenly an unfamiliar police officer shouted at them to get back. Paul shouted back at him and told him they were friends with Stephanie. The police officer didn't care who they knew, as long as they stepped back. Shauna and Paul stepped a few steps back, and still staring down at the mangled car watching the crew trying to rescue her. Shauna took the phone away from Paul and put it to her ear.

"Stephanie!" she shouted. She couldn't hear anything but people talking in a far distance from the phone.

Paul saw them rip open the driver's door with the jaw's of life, and then saw one of the official's reach in. "Stephanie!" she shouted again, and heard the official mention she wasn't wearing a seatbelt

Shauna violently turned off her phone and slammed it into Paul's hand. She watched and waited for the rescue men to get her out of the car, then saw them force the door open wider.

Paul stepped closer to the edge, and saw the stretcher being lowered down. He watched the men carefully pull Stephanie out, and strap her on the stretcher.

"Okay, pull us up!" The official shouted to the top. They started to climb the hill holding on to the stretcher, and making sure Stephanie didn't fall off. Shauna walked closer to the men pulling on the rope, and was again stopped by the same police officer. Paul pushed himself through, and walked over to the ambulance. The police officer grabbed Paul by the shirt of his arm, as Paul swung his arm away almost smacking the officer in the face. The chief saw Paul and Shauna struggling with the officer, and stomped over to them with his hand out.

"What are you two doing here!" he shouted. "You're going to be in the way. Stand back, and let the rescue men do their job!"

"Chief, is she going to be okay?" Shauna asked still trying to push her way through.

"She's being transported to the hospital. You can see her then."

Shauna stepped away, and watched Stephanie get slid into the back of the ambulance. Shauna saw her face and arms full of scrapes and bruises, and her eyes were closed because she was unconscious. She put her hand over her face and started to tear when she thought of the worst. Paul hugged her for a moment as he watched the ambulance starting to roll away.

"Let's follow the ambulance," Paul said, and lightly nudged her to walk to the car. Paul and Shauna heard the siren go off from the ambulance as it sped off down the road. Shauna and Paul walked back to their car still watching the ambulance until it was out of sight.

"I want to know why she went off the road," Shauna told him. "I want to know why now!" She said demanding.

Paul sat there in silence as she drove toward the hospital. He didn't want to say anything to upset her more than she already was. Shauna had only one thought on her mind. The one person that would make Stephanie lose complete control of anything she was doing.

"Mitchell," she thought. "He's the bastard who would make her lose control." Her temper started to flare, her eyes turned mean when she pictured Mitchell's face in her thoughts, and then gripped the steering wheel with all her strength. She thought of how she was going to get hurtful revenge against him for doing this to her best friend.

6

Shauna stood in front of Stephanie's hospital room looking at her through the window on the door. Steph was lying comatose in the bed. Her head was all bandaged up, and her arms were covered with needles and sensor pads. The machines next to her monitored her life, and when, or if, she was going to come out of the coma she slipped into.

Shauna was scared. She felt helpless and lost. She didn't want her best friend to die. The doctor told her father that she had suffered bad head injuries in the accident, and the only thing they can do is wait and hope she comes out of the coma.

Mitchell was nowhere in sight, and Shauna didn't really want to see him anyway, or she would kill him in a heartbeat. Paul put his arms around her to give her a little comfort, for him or for her; he really didn't know. All he wanted to do was to be held from someone right now, but Shauna quickly moved away from him, she didn't want any comfort from anyone, and she didn't want to be touched.

Paul shrugged her attitude off and walked over to the phone, and picked up the receiver. He turned around and glared at her for a moment, then dialed his home phone number. Stephanie's father came over and stood next to Shauna. They didn't say anything, they didn't have to. They just looked through the window and prayed she was going to be okay. Shauna glanced over at Paul talking with his mother explaining to her what had happened. She could hear it in his voice he was upset, but didn't want to show it in front of anyone. He told his mother he would be home soon since there was nothing he could do but wait until Stephanie woke up. He hung up the phone and walked back to where Shauna and Stephanie's father were, and for a brief moment in time, they all silently stared at Stephanie through the glass buried in their own thoughts of how it all happened.

"Shauna, I think we should go home and come back tomorrow. There's nothing we can do but wait," Paul told her.

"Shauna, I think Paul is right," Stephanie's father spoke. "You should go home and get some rest." Shauna looked at him, and thought for a moment of how she wanted to be by her side hopefully when she wakes up. But she also knew it could be days, months, or even years before she opens her eyes.

She put her arms around Stephanie's father and gave him a hug. "Call me if anything changes with her," she told him. "You have my cell number."

"I will, don't worry." Shauna and Paul walked away still feeling lost, and just before they walked through the doors, Shauna looked back one more time and smiled at her father.

They walked out of the hospital and headed toward the car, when they saw Mitchell walking toward them. Shauna's face turned beat red as the anger built up inside, and wouldn't take her eyes off of Mitchell. The thought of crushing his skull triggered her adrenalin to explode. Suddenly she stopped and stood there burning her eyes on Mitchell, and dropped her bag. She took off as fast as she could run, and tackled him like a football player down on the cement sidewalk. She punched Mitchell in the face as hard as she could. "You bastard!" she shouted. "You did this to Stephanie! It's your fault!" She shouted again and kept punching him hard in the chest until her strength weakened from sorrow.

"I didn't do anything!" Mitchell shouted back, trying to fight her off, and looked at Paul standing over them. Paul stood there and waited for Shauna to finish taking her aggression out on him. Suddenly Mitchell grabbed Shauna's arms and threw Shauna off of him, and then Paul quickly slammed his foot down on his chest holding him down on the ground.

"She's right. It is your fault she's in a coma. It's your fault she smashed up her car," He told him. "You're such an asshole. What the hell happened to you? I don't want to see you around anymore." Mitchell relaxed himself on the cement and waited for Paul to take his foot off his chest. Shauna was crying as she went back and picked up her bag. Paul and Mitchell stared at each other for a moment as Paul waited for Shauna. He took his foot of Mitchell's chest, and let him get to his feet.

"Why don't you go home?" Shauna told him and pushed him as Mitchell caught himself before he fell. "There's no reason for you to be here,"

"Stephanie came over to my house today and we broke up," Mitchell said.

"Good!" Shauna screamed as loud as she could and glanced around at all the people watching them. Shauna pulled Paul by the hand and dragged him toward the car.

"It's not over!" Mitchell shouted at them. "It's not over…. Not just yet," he whispered to himself and watched them jump in the car and drive away. He didn't like the fact that Shauna blamed her accident on him. He didn't like it when his so called best friend just stood there, and let his bitchy girlfriend continuously punch him. Mitchell put his hand on his jaw and thought of Shauna's lighting speed fist hammering him. He had the idea they were all going to be friends until the very end. He never dreamed of anything else, he never wanted to.

Paul and Shauna drove down the street in silence. Paul noticed the sun was setting and looked at the orange sky. He smiled and knew tomorrow was going to be a hot one. The thoughts of telling Mitchell he didn't want to see him anymore bothered him a lot. In fact, he regretted saying every word.

Shauna drove by the place where Stephanie went off the road as she slowed the car down, and looked down at the tree where her car slammed into. She pulled her car over and got out, and walked over to the broken guard rail staring at the tree from the road. The highway department placed orange cones where she went through the barrier, and the tree was ripped apart from her car. Paul sat there in the car, and listened to the radio with his eyes closed trying to forget the day even happened.

Shauna decided she was going to walk down the hill and look at the tree even closer. She slid down the hill on her feet, and followed Stephanie's tire tracks to the tree. She looked at the tree and saw the bark had been completely ripped away from its trunk. She realized Stephanie was lucky the tree was there. It saved her from possibly being swept away and drowning in the fast moving river.

She looked up toward the road, and saw a glimpse of a man with a black shroud staring down at her. She got the willies thinking it was the grim reaper. She started to walk up the hill still looking at the man when she slipped down on the grass. She caught her balance and looked up again and noticed the man was gone.

"Shauna," she heard a voice whispering through the air. Chills quickly went up and down her spine as she stopped and looked around the hill. She wondered where the voice was coming from, and looked for the man with the black shroud. "Shauna," She heard the voice again. She forced herself up the hill, and ran across the street to the car.

Paul still had his eyes closed listening to the music as she put it into gear and drove off. She saw the man again in the rear view mirror, and thought maybe she was tired and her eyes and ears were playing tricks on her.

Paul opened his eyes feeling the car moving, and realized he dozed off for a few moments. He glanced over at Shauna yawning, and looking like she was ready for a nap.

"We'll be home in a minute. I'm going to drop you off, and then I'm going to go home and sleep," Shauna told him. Paul didn't really have the energy to argue with her, so he agreed to get out when she stopped the car.

Shauna came to a skidding halt when she pulled up to Paul's house. He kissed her, and quickly jumped out of the car. Shauna drove off down the road looking in the rear view mirror at Paul. She thought of Stephanie, and pictured in her mind what she could have possibly gone through when she lost control of her car.

Suddenly she saw the man with the black shroud in her rear view mirror again. She blinked her eyes and looked again to make sure she wasn't seeing things.

"Shauna," she heard her name being whispered. She looked down at the radio and shut it off. "Shauna," she heard her name again. Now she was really frightened, and looked around the back seat. "Shauna," she heard her name again. She looked at the road, and saw the man with the black shroud right in front of her. She slammed on her brakes, closed her eyes hoping she wouldn't hit him, and slid the car right through the man. When car came to a quick stop she opened her eyes and slowly pulled the car over to the side of the road. Frightened as she was, she got out of the car and looked around and didn't see anyone. She bent down and looked under the car fearing the worst, and when she stood up she saw the man with the black shroud standing over her. "Shauna," the voice said, as he slowly started to take the hood off his head.

She stepped back waiting to see who he was as the chills came back. Shauna stood there and froze when she saw the horrible face. She knew it was the Dark Mountain Phantom. She became terrified, she tried to run. She tried to move but she couldn't. She felt like a force, or some kind of spell had come over her body and became a prisoner in her own self.

The man she saw was nobody, he had no identity. His eyes were hollow and black as night. His face was thickly covered with drooling blood that slowly oozed out of deep craters in his face down to the neckline.

"You have my eyes." the Phantom said and floated closer to her. Shauna wanted to scream. She wanted to run, and still, she couldn't move a muscle. She looked into the Phantoms mouth and saw nothing but blackness. "I want my eyes." the Phantom said louder. Shauna saw the Phantoms boney fingers slowly coming out from inside the shroud. They were as pointy as a needle, fragile, and yet long and as strong as a kitchen knife.

Her eyes filled up with tears. The Phantom's pointy fingers slowly came closer to her eyes and touched her cheeks. She felt the sharp points touching the bottom of her eyes as they pressed against her forcing her eyes to protrude outward. She started to scream when she felt the points dig into the bottom of her eyeballs. She knew the Phantom was going to take her life, and she knew she couldn't do anything about it. Underneath the excruciating pain, she thought of her family, Paul, Stephanie, and how she was going to miss them all. Unexpectedly she heard a car slow down and stopped next to her.

"Are you alright Miss?" The woman asked from the car and wondered why she was standing stiff as a board with her head tilted upward in tears. The Phantom caught the shiny reflection of the passenger side mirror and quickly disappeared. Shauna suddenly could move again, as she quickly fell to the ground shaking like a leaf, terrified, and realizing that the Dark Mountain Phantom had vanished from her presence. She started to cry out loud still feeling the pain in her eyes. The Phantom was taking her life, and no one but her could see him. The woman pulled over to the side of the road worried and wondering what was happening, and ran over to Shauna.

"Are you okay? Do you need some help?" She asked.

"I'm fine. I'm fine," Shauna replied. "I just need to sit for a moment, and gather my thoughts. Thank you for stopping though." Shauna continued to sob loudly with her hands over her eyes.

"Are you sure you're alright?" the woman asked again concerned.

Shauna just shook her head keeping her hands pressed against her eyes, and leaned against her car. The woman slowly stood back up, and waited a moment before she went back to her own car. The woman took no chances. She picked up her cell phone and called the police anyway. Shauna waved to the woman as the woman drove away. She sat there for a few more minutes realizing that the legend of Dark Mountain was utterly real, and the Phantom was nothing what she had expected.

She quickly jumped to her feet, opened the door and sat in her car. She looked into her rear view mirror still shaking like a leaf, and tried to smile when she saw the empty road behind her. She quickly drove off down the road, and saw a police cruiser with its lights flashing quickly coming the other way. She kept driving toward home as the cruiser passed at high speed. She wiped her eyes and looked back in the mirror waiting for the police to turn around and stop her.

They didn't, and she was relieved they didn't. She wondered if the lady that wanted to help her called the police, or were they just going to another call. She didn't care, she didn't want to care. She just wanted to go home.

　　She thought about the terrifying experience she just went through, and wondered what the Phantom meant when he said he wanted his eyes. Her mind was spinning, thinking, and pounding. She was scared of everything and didn't understand why. She suddenly remembered Paul's mother telling the story about the emeralds, and how they were the Phantom's eyes. Then she thought of Mitchell holding the emeralds in his hands.

　　"That bastard!" she shouted. "He has the emeralds! God, I hate him so much!" She turned the corner and headed for Paul's house to tell him what happened. This time Shauna wanted someone to hold. She wanted someone to calm her down and make the nightmare go away.

7

Mitchell stood in front of Stephanie's door, and looked at her all banged up. He glanced over at her father sitting near the water fountain with his legs and arms crossed, and pretty much trying to ignore Mitchell with his head down stuck in a magazine. He turned back with a nasty smile across his face staring through the window. "She deserves what she got for breaking up with me," he said unsympathetically.

He stared at her for a moment looking at all the bandages wrapped around her head, the tubes attached to her arm, and walked away thinking she wouldn't be here if he didn't let her leave. "Oh well," he thought as he pushed open the door to leave. He walked down the sidewalk remembering Paul and his bitchy ball and chain smacking him around then jumped over the small hedges to his car.

"Mitchell," he heard his name echoing through the air. He looked around and didn't see anyone but an old man in a wheel chair slumped over, and being pushed by a nurse. He unlocked the door to his car, and glanced around the parking lot one more time wondering who said his name before he jumped in. He turned the key to start his car but nothing happened, nothing at all. He tried it again, and still, nothing but silence. Rolling his eyes and getting frustrated, he popped the hood of the car, and jumped out to take a look. He noticed the battery cable was frayed from the battery post, and squeezed it together. He jumped in and turned the key as the engine quickly started. He jumped back out and shut the hood thinking to himself, he better go right now and have it looked at.

He drove down the road toward his friend the mechanic when he ran over a big pothole going over Woodland Bridge, and the car went completely dead. He slammed his hand on the steering wheel and rolled the car to the side of the road cursing and swearing, and popped the hood again.

He squeezed the wires together not realizing the wires were hot and burned his fingers and thumb. "Mitchell," he heard his name whisper through the air. He quickly turned his head and looked around. "Mitchell," He heard his name again. He looked down the road, and saw a tall man with a black shroud standing in the middle. He stared at the man for a moment and tried to recognize who he was, and then noticed the man was floating in midair. Mitchell thought maybe someone was playing tricks on him, or his eyes were just tired as he walked closer to the man.

Suddenly, Mitchell watched as the man vanished right in front of him. Mitchell stopped and looked around. He got frightened and started to yell and swear at the man. He turned around to head back to his car when unexpectedly saw the Phantom standing over him just inches away. Mitchell's eye's widened. He couldn't believe what he was seeing. He tried to run but much to his surprise, he couldn't move. His body was completely frozen. He pushed himself to move harder but nothing happened. The Phantom slowly floated closer to Mitchell, and slowly took off his hood. Mitchell stared at the hollow eyes and saw his terrifying bloody face.

"Mitchell," the Phantom whispered. "I want my eyes."

Mitchell tried to close his eyes in fear and saw the Phantoms long pointed fingers come out of his shroud and coming closer to him. "Who are you? I don't have your eyes," he wanted to tell the Phantom and felt the cold boney fingers against his cheeks.

"I want my eyes Mitchell," the Phantom whispered again louder.

Mitchell felt his boney fingers push against the bottom of his eyes. He wanted to tell him badly he didn't have them but he couldn't.

"Where are my eyes Mitchell?" the Phantom shouted in a deep scary tone and slowly pressed harder. Mitchell's eyes started to bug out of his sockets. He could feel the points of the Phantom's fingers pushing up inside his eyes.

Mitchell's sight suddenly went black, and wanted to scream as the pain was unbearable. Suddenly, the Phantom pushed harder into his eyes and pulled them out of the sockets with the blood veins rapidly snapping off from the eyeball. Mitchell tried to scream as loud as he could as he felt the shooting excruciating pain. The Phantom took the eyes. He could sense they weren't his eyes and he got angry and started yelling that deep yell. Mitchell heard the Phantom's ear piercing scream and remembered the yelling he heard on the mountain. The Phantom pulled his other long pointed boney hand from his shroud, grabbed Mitchell by the side of the head, and slowly twisted his neck around until it snapped like a branch. Mitchell's dead body fell to the ground and laid there on the side of the road with blood oozing out of his eye sockets. The Phantom carefully slid Mitchell's eyes off his fingers letting them fall, and roll up against Mitchell's shoulder. After that, the Phantom quickly disappeared into thin air.

Mitchell lay dead on the side of the road for a long while until a single car drove by and the driver saw him on the ground. The car quickly stopped as a male driver jumped out and ran over to Mitchell to see if he was okay. He put his hand on his shoulder and suddenly felt wetness on his fingers. The man looked down and noticed he had touched something round. He picked one of them up and looked closely at the slimy filmy bloody ball. The man looked at Mitchell's face and saw the dried blood on his cheeks and then noticed his eyes were missing, and then realized he was holding one in his hand.

The man quickly jumped away from Mitchell, tossed his slimy eyeball back on the ground and ran back to his car wiping his fingers on his pants. He grabbed his cell phone and violently threw up all down the side of his car. He tried to dial 9-1-1 and threw up again on the ground. Finally, he dialed the number and told the dispatcher about Mitchell. He couldn't look over at Mitchell anymore thinking he might throw up again, and waited for the police to arrive. He sat in his car thinking to himself, he never should have pulled over, and then put his hand on his stomach and closed his eyes leaning against the seat.

8

Paul woke up to a slamming knock of his bedroom door. He slid off his bed and when he opened the door he saw Shauna full of tears shaking like a leaf.

"What's the matter?" he asked walking over to give her a hug

She stood there crying uncontrollably in his arms and unable to stop and tell him what happened on the side of the road. He smiled at her almost to the point of laughing when she hauled off and slapped him in the face.

"What the hell was that for?" he shouted, watching her push by him and sat on his bed.

"I almost got killed out on the road today, because I met up with the Dark Mountain Phantom," she spat at him and crossed her arms and looked toward the wall.

"What?" he said confused. "What are you saying?"

"The Phantom had his long pointy fingers digging in my eyes until some lady stopped and asked me if I was alright." She wiped the tears rolling down her face still looking at the wall.

Paul went over and sat down next to her, and listened to her story knowing she wasn't kidding around. He rubbed the side of his face where she slapped him, and felt a slight burning sensation.

"We need to find those stupid emeralds and give them back to the mountain," she told him.

"Mitchell is the one who's had them the whole time, and as far as he's concerned we can just go pound sand."

"Paul, if we don't give back the stones, he's going to kill me, you, and everybody else until he finds them."

"Then we'll get them back. But first, let's go tell my mother what happened to you."

They walked down the stairs and went into the kitchen where Paul's mother was sitting at the table reading the newspaper.

"Hi Jess," Shauna said quietly.

Paul's mother looked up and saw the red mark on Paul's face. She wondered why Shauna had slapped him, and then wondered if Paul was trying to do something he shouldn't have.

"Mom, we need to talk," Paul said and sat down putting his elbows on the table.

"Why do you have a red mark on your face?" his mother asked.

"I slapped him to get his attention," Shauna told her.

"Shauna just had a close encounter with the Dark Mountain Phantom," Paul said.

His mother dropped the paper on the table. Her eyes widened and her mouth dropped. She knew exactly what they were talking about, and knew the Phantom will come back again to look for his eyes. "When did you see him?" she asked.

"When I thought I saw a man in the middle of the road, and I slammed on my brakes thinking I was going to hit him."

Paul's mother listened and tried to calm herself down from her own frightening memories. "Did you freeze when he was standing over you?" she asked.

"Yes, I did," Shauna said nervously

Paul's mother knew she was almost in the last stage before he ripped her eyes out of her head. The phone rang and startled everyone. Paul jumped up and answered it. He heard a man's voice on the other end and couldn't distinguish who he was.

"This is Chief William Parsons," the man said on the other line.

Paul handed the phone to his mother. "Hello?" she said.

"Jess, it's Billy," he said.

"Hi Billy," she answered him.

"Jess, I have some tragic news. Mitchell's…. His…. Jessica, Paul's friend Mitchell is dead," he told her

She dropped her mouth and put her hand on her chest when Billy was explaining the detail's to her. She relived the memories of her best friend in her thoughts, and how the Phantom took her life. Her eyes filled up with tears. She knew this was as real as much as it was when she was young. She shut the phone off and looked at Shauna and Paul. "I have something I need to tell you," she said calmly.

Paul and Shauna waited for her to catch her thoughts and tell them what had happened.

"Mitchell is no longer with us," she told them and put her head down.

Shauna and Paul sat there in silence, and tried to absorb what she just told them. Paul's gut turned upside down knowing they've been friends since he doesn't know when. Shauna had nothing to say. She remembered Mitchell always being an asshole, and didn't like him in the least bit. She looked at Paul's mother and uncaringly shrugged her shoulders.

Paul still couldn't get it to sink in that Mitchell was dead, and remembered the last words he said to him

"How did he die?" Shauna asked not really caring but she needed to know.

"The Phantom did it," she told her.

Even though, Paul's mother told them the story about the Dark Mountain Phantom. Paul still couldn't understand how Mitchell had died. Paul's mother explained the situation further so Paul could understand how Mitchell died. Paul slumped down in his chair. Still, he couldn't comprehend that his friend for so many years was really dead, in some case he wouldn't let it sink in.

Shauna stood up from the table and put her hand on Paul's shoulder. She looked over at Paul's mother one more time, and then walked into the other room. Her mind was full of fear since she's already had the unexpected thrill of meeting the Phantom face to face. She had a strong funny feeling she was going to be the next one to die.

Paul walked into the other room and saw Shauna crying quietly. He knew everything about the Dark Mountain was bothering her, but he had no idea of the pain she was going through. Shauna looked at Paul and without a word from either of them, she went over and hugged him tight and put her head down on his chest.

"What are we going to do now about the emeralds?" she asked.

Paul rubbed her back with a blank thought. He didn't know what to do, or where he should even start. He thought about Mitchell and wondered where he had put the stones. He knew Mitchell wouldn't put them in a secure place since his room was always a trash pit, and his mother finally after fifteen years of wasting her breath, gave up trying to get him to clean it up.

"We need to go break into his room and find the emeralds," he told her.

Shauna backed away from him, and looked at him and thought about what he just said. "No we can't, it will be too dangerous, we'll get caught," she said and headed for the stairs.

"We won't get caught. We'll just climb the back fence, and jump on the roof next to his window. I've done it a million times."

"That's when you guys were kids. Now you just wait for him in the car. When was the last time you were in his room?" Shauna asked hoping he will realize it's all different know since he got older.

"It's been a while, but I'm sure everything is still the same. We'll just tell Mom we're going out for a little while, okay."

"Fine, but let's just make it quick," she insisted.

Shauna walked upstairs to Paul's bedroom and picked up her bag hanging off the side of the bed. Paul went back to the kitchen and told his mother where they were going. Shauna jumped off the last step thinking Paul was already in the car waiting for her when she opened the door, and unexpectedly saw the Dark Mountain Phantom. She screamed as loud as she could before the Phantom put a hold on her.

"Shauna," the Phantom whispered.

Paul and his mother came dashing out of the kitchen and saw Shauna standing completely still and couldn't move. Paul saw the Phantom and stopped in his tracks not knowing what to do. His mother ran past Paul, and pushed Shauna to the ground and slammed the door. She couldn't see the Phantom, but she knew he was there. The Phantom came through the door and pulled the shroud over his head.

"Where are my eyes!" the Phantom said angrily and leaned down toward Shauna. She stared into his black hollow eyes. She tried to scream, but the Phantom still had a hold of her body. Paul's mother looked at her lying there with her eyes wide open and staring over her shoulder. She could feel the evil presence of the Phantom behind her. She quickly got to her feet and dragged Shauna by the shirt, pulling her to the other side of the room. Shauna still was hypnotized and frozen. Paul still stood there and looked on and unable to get a hold of him self and help Shauna. He couldn't believe the stories he was told years ago actually became true.

Shauna's eyes were starting to pop out of her sockets when Paul's mother put her hand over her eyes praying she wouldn't die in her arms. Suddenly she remembered her friend Billy telling her years ago that a mirror will stop the Phantom for a brief moment. She looked up at the wall and saw the small oval mirror over the couch. She took her shoe off her foot, and threw it against the mirror as hard as she could and causing it to smash all over the couch. She quickly ran over and grabbed a big piece and placed it in front of Shauna's eyes. The reflection startled the Phantom and took his pointed his fingers away from Shauna.

"Where are my eyes?" The Phantom screamed. "Where are my eyes?" the Phantom said disappearing into thin air.

Shauna started to hyperventilate as Paul fainted, and fell to the floor. Paul's mother tossed the mirror away from Shauna's eyes and sat down on the floor next to her. She looked over at Paul and started to laugh to hide her own fear. Shauna rubbed her eyes and felt the pain once again on the bottom of her eyelids.

"He wants me dead doesn't he?" she asked catching her breath.

"He wants the emeralds. He wants his eyes," she told her and looked at the broken mirror on the wall. She glanced down and noticed she had cut herself across the palm of her hand. Shauna slowly took her hand and squeezed it into hers. She wanted to thank her for saving her life but she couldn't say the words. Paul's mother cracked a smile and nodded her head as though she did say the words.

Shauna looked over at Paul moving around on the floor trying to regain consciousness. She crawled over to him and lay on top of him. She thought about the emeralds in Mitchell's house and looked over at Paul's mother still sitting on the floor.

"Paul, are you okay?" Shauna asked.

"Yeah, I'm fine. I must have fainted or something," He replied.

"Paul," his mother spoke. "You did faint, and the reason you fainted is because you saw the Phantom for the first time."

"Yes I did, but I don't remember anything after that."

Paul's mother got off the floor, walked back to the kitchen, and reached for the phone. She dialed the police station and waited for the dispatcher to answer. The phone kept ringing and ringing. She hung up the phone and dialed it again. The dispatcher answered the phone. "Police emergency your call is being recorded," she heard a man's voice and not of Sheila who has been at the police department for more than twenty five years.

"Hello," she heard the man's voice again. "Yes," she answered. "Could I speak to Bill Parsons?"

"One moment please."

She waited and waited. Five minutes went by and her friend Billy never came on. Five more minutes went by and still, she waited. Finally, Billy came on the phone as she heard him say hello, but to her, something in his voice told her didn't sound like Billy. "Billy?" she asked.

"Jessica," she heard as a whisper. Chills went up and down her spine when she heard the evil sound of her name. She quickly clicked off the phone and ran into the living room.

"Paul, where are the stones?" she asked.

"Mitchell had them. I don't know where they would be?" he answered her.

"We need to go over to his house. Go to the car we're going now," she demanded.

Paul and Shauna went to the door and slowly opened it up. They looked out expecting to see the Phantom again, but they only saw the everyday things in the yard. They ran to the car frightened and worried. They saw Paul's mother run out, jump in, and screeched the tires out of the driveway. She floored the accelerator toward Mitchell's house as the thoughts of what to do, and how to get the stones ran through her mind.

When she rounded the corner they saw cars lined up on each side of the road. Paul, Shauna, and his mother all wondered why so many cars were at Mitchell's home if he was only found dead just a few hours before. She stopped in the middle of the road, jumped out of the car leaving the door wide open, and ran up to the house and rang the door bell.

Mitchell's mother answered the door wearing a black dress and her face was covered over with a black net. She stood there and looked at Paul's mother and didn't say a word. Paul's mother wanted to ask her if she can to go up to Mitchell's room and find the emerald's, but she could find the right reason in her head, so she apologized for the loss of her son and then calmly walked away.

"We're going to see Billy," Paul's mother said. "I'm going to talk to him about everyone who has seen the Phantom."

"Mom, we're the only ones who has seen the Phantom," Paul said.

"No Paul, there is a lot more people in this town that has seen the Phantom than just you, a lot more."

They drove by the old stores on Main Street heading for the police station, when Paul's mother looked over and saw an old man with dark sun glasses sitting on the park bench. She remembered an old man telling her about the mountain, and strangely wondered if it was the same man. Suddenly she saw the man smile at her, and didn't realize the car was veering into on coming traffic.

"Mom, look out!" Paul screamed as his mother turned her head and straightened out the car. Suddenly they heard a police siren in back of them as she looked in the rear view mirror, and then pulled the car over to the side of the road. The policeman walked over to the car and much to their surprise. It was Paul's mother's friend the chief of police, Billy.

"Thank God it's you," she said and relaxed in her seat. I tried to call you earlier," she mentioned.

"When, today?" he asked.

"Yes just a little while ago. I called the station and some man answered the phone."

"A man, we don't have a man dispatcher?" He said confused. You must have dialed the wrong number."

"Mmm, I don't know maybe I did." She said, but she was sure to herself she dialed the right number.

"Anyway Jessica, fancy driving skills I see," Bill said sarcastically and leaned against the driver's door smiling up a storm.

The Phantom is back again Billy," she said ignoring his comment.

Billy stepped back and stared into her eyes. He remembered seeing Mitchell on the side of the road, and remembered talking about it over her house, but it really didn't sink in that the Dark Mountain Phantom was awake again until Jessica said those words to him.

"Where are the stones?" he asked.

"Mitchell was the one who took them," Shauna told him.

Paul's mother looked over at the old man still sitting on the park bench with a smile across his face. She still had that feeling it was the same old man when she was a young girl.

"Billy," she said and pointed her finger toward the card store. "That old man who is sitting over there on the park bench, is he the same old man we saw that told us the story about the Dark Mountain?" she asked.

Billy looked behind him, and searched for the old man sitting. He knew who she was talking about, but he couldn't see him anywhere.

"Jess, I don't see him. Where are you looking?" He covered his eyes from the sun's glare.

"He's sitting right there in front of the card store," she told him.

"Jessica, I still don't see him."

Paul's mother suddenly got an eerie feeling. She didn't know what to say to Billy since she realized she was the only one who could see the old man. She opened the door and got out of the car. She looked at Billy without saying a word and walked across the street to toward old man. Billy stayed with Shauna and Paul as they watched where she was going. Jessica slowly walked up to the old man and stared at him for a moment.

The old man sat there still holding this, never ending smile across his face. Paul's mother still wondered if he was the same man. "He looks the same?" she thought. "The glasses are the same, and his cane seems familiar?"

The old man turned his head and looked at her. "You know who I am Jessica," he whispered softly. He slowly reached up to his sunglasses and pulled them off his face. Paul's mother quickly jumped back a bit, when she saw the old man had no eyes. She wanted to scream and run, but her curiosity stopped her from going anywhere.

Billy, Shauna, and Paul still watched on, seeing only her as she stood next to the park bench. They didn't know what she was doing, but they watched closely and wondered if anything was going to happen.

Paul's mother just stared at the black empty eyes on the old man.

"He's looking for his eyes Jessica," the old man whispered again. "It's just like before, you give him his eyes back, and he'll leave everyone alone."

"Who are you?" she asked.

"I'm the man who sees things," he chuckled a bit and smiled again as he vanished before her.

She walked back to the car, and then looked back one more time at the bench.

"Are you alright Jess?" Billy asked thinking she just saw a ghost.

"I'm fine, but we need to find the emeralds before he kills everyone, including my only son.

9

Stephanie twitched continuously and her heart rate rapidly increased on the monitor when she started coming out of her coma. Her father eyes began to fill up with tears when he was told she was going to be okay.

He called all the people close to his daughter, and when he called Mitchell's mother he heard the tragic news that Mitchell was dead. He hung up the phone and realized he needed to tell Stephanie what happened. But he didn't want to tell her until she was strong enough to withstand the terrible shock. He walked into her room and watched her slowly open her eyes. She tried to smile and squeeze his hand when she saw her father holding hers, but she felt the skin on her face was feeling a little tight like a sun burn, and slightly hurt.

The nurse came in and checked her over. Doctor Metagaham came in to see her. He waved his little flashlight in her eyes and felt her skin for warmth. He smiled at her father and adjusted the machine behind him. "I think she's going to be doing jumping jacks in no time at all," he said.

"What happened to me Daddy?" Stephanie asked in a low whisper and noticed her mouth was completely dry.

"Let's just say you went to sleep for a while," Doctor Metagaham spoke up.

"We'll talk about it later, and after you get back on your feet," her father said.

"I'm wicked thirsty. Can I have some water?" she asked snapping her tongue off of the roof of her mouth.

The nurse poured her a cold cup of water with small ice chips inside, and helped her take a sip. Stephanie put her hand over her head and felt all the bandages. She still couldn't comprehend why she was in the hospital, and took another sip of the cold water.

"Well," The doctor spoke. "We need to let Stephanie rest for a while, so…."

Her father looked at the doctor with a little irritation since she just woke up from almost death, and decided to agree with him. He let her hand go and gave her a kiss on the cheek. "I'll see you soon. Try to get some rest," he told her.

Stephanie smiled as much as she could and waved goodbye. She watched her father walk out the door and then closed her eyes.

She slowly started remembering the tree she slammed into, and quickly opened her eyes in fright. She looked around the room breathing heavy. The nurse came over and took her by the hand.

"It was a car accident. That's why I'm here, right?" Stephanie asked.

"Yes, it was. You were in a bad car accident. You almost died," The nurse told her as she watched Stephanie slowly close her eyes again.

Stephanie started remembering the day step by step, and then remembered when her car went over the embankment. The nurse held her hand until she was calmed down. Suddenly she saw Mitchell running after her with his hands in the air. "It's not over," she shouted loudly and opened her eyes again

"What's not over?" the nurse asked.

"Mitchell, he's coming for me. I think he's going to kill me for breaking up with him," she said in hysterics.

"It's alright," the nurse said and reached over and pushed the button for more assistance. The doctor quickly rushed in with another nurse and noticed Stephanie was shaking and breathing heavy.

"Nurse what happened?" he asked.

"I don't know doctor. She started to think about someone named Mitchell," she told him.

"Mitchell, Mitchell is, or was my boyfriend," Stephanie said frantic. "I broke up with him the same day I crashed my car. He's going to come after me I can feel it."

"Shh, everything is alright," the doctor said calmly. "Nobody is going to come after you. You're safe with us." In the back of his mind he remembered someone by the name of Mitchell was wheeled in dead from the side of the road earlier in the week. He stuck Stephanie with a sleeping sedative and watched her close her eyes for the last time and drift into never land. He watched her for a moment with a smile. He slowly walked out of her room the same time the nurse reached over and shut the light off. Stephanie fell into a deep relaxing sleep, and started dreaming of her adventure in the Dark Mountain, and Mitchell.

She saw the stones in Mitchell's hands as he waved them back and forth sitting in front of the campfire. She saw a tall man quietly standing in back of him a short distance away. He wore a black shroud. He was floating ghostly in mid air and slowly coming closer to Mitchell. She watched Mitchell with a greedy smile on his face as he played with the stones, unaware of anything else. She saw the man reach up and slowly pull his hood over his head as he smiled looking down at Mitchell. His face was drooling with blood down on the top of Mitchell's head, and his eyes were as black as night.

She screamed as loud as she could to warn Mitchell, but he didn't hear a sound. Mitchell stopped playing with the stone's when he felt something drip on his head. He put his hand on his head, and looked up to see what was dripping. He saw a dark shadow standing over him, but he couldn't see who it was.

The Phantom smiled at Stephanie before he placed his long boney hands down on his face and tear Mitchell's eyes out from its sockets. Stephanie screamed in fear when she saw the Phantom take Mitchell's head and twist it until his neck cracked like the shell of a walnut, and threw his dead body into the burning fire

She screamed again as she saw Mitchell's body ignite into a ball of flame and reach into the sky. Suddenly she felt herself running as fast as she could, and stopped when she reached the edge of the dark forest feeling her head pounding with pain. She put her hands on her head and felt a deep cut across her hairline slowly following her fingers across the stitches.

"Come inside," she heard a deep evil whisper through the forest. She looked around and saw the Phantom waving his boney fingers at her to come in. She slowly walked into the forest, deeper and deeper she walked until she saw nothing but glowing eyes shifting in all directions. She saw the hanging ropes dangling from the trees.

"Why are these ropes here?" she asked and heard her own voice echo through the forest.

"They're here for you Stephanie," she heard the Phantom's deep voice whisper.

Stephanie felt the rope fall around her neck and slowly tighten. Suddenly she was yanked off her feet hanging ten feet in the air. She felt the rope squeeze tighter and tighter as her body dangled helplessly. She started gasping for air and pulling against the rope with her fingers and kicked her feet. She wanted to breathe but the rope kept getting tighter and tighter as she wiggled and panicked.

She wiggled and pulled with all her might against the rope trying to break free. Then, she quickly felt her strength in her hands weakened. Her eyes quickly went bloodshot from the lack of oxygen, and her fingers became numb. Slowly she dropped her arms down to her sides limp, helpless, and numb, as her eyes rolled back behind her eye lids. She felt herself drifting away and giving up on life. She drifted further and further feeling her heart rate slowly coming to a stop. She knew she was dieing as a single tear fell from her eye and rolled down her cheek and onto the pillow.

Shauna, Paul, and her mother walked into the room. Paul clicked on the light and looked at Stephanie sleeping. Shauna looked at Stephanie and saw the tear line on her cheek and realized something was wrong. She quickly went over and felt the skin on her face. "Paul, get some help she's not breathing!" she yelled.

Paul ran out of the room and screaming for someone to help. Suddenly two doctors and three nurses rushed into the room, and quickly worked on Stephanie trying to revive her. The life monitor was almost at a straight line, and her heart rate was dropping fast. The doctor put an oxygen mask on Stephanie as Shauna and Paul stepped away and watched in worry thinking she's not going to make it.

A nurse turned around and escorted them out of the room and shut the door. They all watched as the doctor's and nurse's pumped her chest and shocked her with an electrical current. Shauna looked over at the monitor and saw the straight line and burst out crying and put her head on Paul's shoulder. Paul and his mother watched and realized there was probably no hope for her now.

"Wait," Paul said. The machine, it's moving again!" he shouted.

Shauna quickly looked up and saw the doctors standing there looking at her carefully. "She's alive. She's alive!" Shauna shouted with joy and hugged Paul.

One of the doctors came out of the room with a phony smile.

"She's back," he said. "This time she'll be watched closely until she feels better. The sedative we induced her with, she had an allergic reaction to it. The medication swelled up her throat preventing her from breathing." he told them. "Her head injury is also worse than we anticipated, so she's going to stay a little longer than I thought."

Shauna didn't care what happened to her best friend, all she cared about was that she was alive, and she was going to okay. She wanted to run in and give her best friend a hug. She knew she couldn't, but in time she knew she would be.

Paul squeezed Shauna close and nudged her over to sit down in the waiting room. His mother stood there, scared and frightened. She had a strong feeling it wasn't just the head injury, or the allergic reaction to the medication. She wanted to believe the Dark Mountain Phantom had everything to do with it. She knew what the Phantom was doing and why. She remembered everything what happened to her and her friends years ago, and knew the Phantom wasn't going to stop until he had the stones.

"Where," she asked herself. "Where," she repeated as the thoughts kept running through her mind.

10

Chief Billy drove down the street in his restored midnight metallic navy blue 1961 Chrysler police cruiser toward the old Glencliff Cemetery where his mother and childhood friends were buried, including his high school girlfriend Paula Sue with his infant son. It's been over seven years since he's seen her, or the spot where she lays deep in the ground. She was the girl he wanted to marry. She was the girl he wanted to die together with at a ripe old age. Now, she was the girl he wants to forget. To this day he never spoke of her since the funeral, or how she died from complications when she was giving birth to his still born son. Billy almost put himself in the nut house after the tragedy and sorrow. Then, he went to the police academy for eleven weeks and straightened himself out..

Jessica didn't know anything about Paula Sue, or he didn't think she did anyway. But for some reason women have this strange way of knowing about things, even if no one tells them anything. For some reason, they just know.

He slowly pulled into the cemetery for his monthly visit to his mother's grave and sometimes he would stop at Lou's place of rest and talk to him about what he's been doing, and how much he misses his best friend. He looked over at Lou's plot and thought about how they use to jump off the Kancamagus Highway cliffs into the freezing cold water, and smiled as the images of Lou's smile came into his mind.

He stopped in front of the big tree where his mother was laid to rest six years ago. He kept that horrible attack tucked away in the back of his head, and thought to him self every time he sees her stone. "Someday that bastard who broke into my mother's home and stole her life that rainy night, will pay for what he did."

73.

He thought of pushing the assailant into an eighteen wheeler's path and watching the blood from his body dragged across the black top for miles. But his thought of pulling the trigger of his gun, as the barrel rested on the bridge of the thug's nose was more realistic every time he reached down to his side and felt the cold black steal in his fingers.

The Chief sat there in the car seat for a moment looking around, and collected thoughts of his mother when she was still alive. He reached for the single yellow rose lying on the passenger seat he bought for his monthly visit, and wondered why his little sister never came with him to visit. He made a mental note he was going to drag her along next month and have her say hi to her own mother, which she intolerably hated, but he didn't care. She was family and that was that.

He pulled himself out of his car, and walked over to his mother's grave and kneeled down. He pulled out last months dead yellow rose from the small pot buried halfway into the ground, and stuck the fresh one in. He prayed for a moment, and asked God for strength to carry on with his own life and hopefully someday change everything and move away. He talked awhile with his mother, and told her he decided he wanted to resign as chief from the police department, because he was sick and tired of the same old routine, with some excitement, but it was few and far between.

He turned his head, and looked over at the spot where Lou was buried and decided today he was going to make a small visit and say hello to his pal.

The Phantom unexpectedly came to his mind as he thought about his wishful girlfriend Jessica, and how he loved the smell of her soft perfume when she held him close. He wanted to be with her and comfort her, but he knew he was too shy to say anything. Suddenly the wind became fierce, and the clouds quickly rolled in. Rain started to pour down hard. He stood there feeling the raindrops and looked up at the sky. "Is this you're doing?" he asked God. "Is there a reason to do this on my visit?"

He let the raindrops soak his body for a moment as he slowly walked back to his car. He put his hand on the door handle and turned and looked back at Lou's grave. He decided he still wanted to go and say hi even though the rain was making him cold and wet. He walked through the rain, splashing into the puddles and noticed some strange movement near Lou's grave. He stopped for a few moments looking around the grave, and thought he saw Lou standing there next to it.

The rain stopped as quickly as it started. Billy slowly walked toward the grave with his hand down on his gun somewhat frightened, and thought maybe it was just his imagination getting out of control. But then again, nothing will ever scare him as much as the Dark Mountain Phantom twenty five years ago.

Billy went closer to Lou's grave, and strangely enough he saw the spirit of his best friend Lou. He looked on, staring at his friend as he stood in front of his headstone wearing the same navy blue suit he was buried in, with that same dead rose his mother slid in his pocket just before they closed the casket. Billy wanted to be scared, but he just couldn't.

"Lou, Is that you?" he asked watchfully.

He waited for Lou's voice. He heard nothing.

"Lou," he asked again and waited.

He watched as his friend Lou slowly disappeared into thin air. Billy had chills go up and down his spine, and wondered if his friend would somehow in the future reappear again. "But why?" He asked himself. "Why did he appear now, after all these years?" he asked himself again. As he heard the sound of the wind blowing threw the cemetery hoping his friend would reappear as he waited.

Billy got tired of waiting after an hour looking and hoping his friend would reappear one more time, and decided to leave the cemetery. He walked back to his car, and opened the door

and sat down with a heavy sigh. He looked over at the passenger side thinking of the yellow rose he brought with him, and glanced over at his mother's grave

He drove away looking back at Lou's grave one more time through the rear view mirror and stopped at the front gate. He turned his head thinking of Lou's spirit he saw, and figured it must have been just his wishful imagination to see his best friend one more time for old time sake.

He drove down the road when Sheila came over the radio announcing there was a drowning accident at the Woodland Bridge. He threw on the lights and sped down the road somewhat forgetting about his friend appearing before him. He pulled up to the bridge and saw a man waving his arms around. The Chief stopped the car and jumped out.

The man told Billy he saw someone tangled up in debris near the bottom of the river. Billy looked down from the bridge, and saw the person he was talking about up against the bridge stones, hung up on a broken branch face down. He walked over to the embankment as he heard more sirens of fire trucks and police cars flying up the road.

He glanced over at the broken guard rail, and thought of the young girl they rescued just days ago. He wondered how she was doing and if Jessica has been there since Paul was friends with her. He walked down the embankment following the tire tracks until he reached the river's edge and saw the floating body. "I need some help down here!" he shouted up to the street.

He stepped into the fast moving river and grabbed a hold of the dead body's foot. He turned the body over and noticed it was a dark-skinned woman in her mid thirties.

Another official stepped into the water and grabbed the dead woman from under the arms. They dragged the woman out of the water and laid her down on the grass.

Billy looked at the woman carefully, and realized she's probably been in the water for quite sometime. "Jesus Christ, "he said out loud when he recognized the woman.

"What's the matter Chief? Do you know this woman?" the official asked.

"Yeah, she's Doc Metagaham's ex-wife Vanessa. I went to school with her years ago."

"Do you think he killed her?"

"I don't know. It's too bad. She was a beautiful woman."

The EMT's slid down the hill with a similar slip board they put Stephanie on, and strapped on the woman. The EMT's and Billy carefully carried her up the hill with the rope carefully being pulled from above and tied to the slip board for more assistance. They put her into the ambulance, untied the rope, and covered her over as they all waited for the coroner to arrive.

Billy went over to talk to the other police officer's for a moment to discuss about the death, and they all agreed they should question the doctor about his ex-wife.

The coroner finally arrived over an hour later and moseyed his tired overweight body over to the ambulance with a spit wet chewed cigar sticking out of his mouth. He lifted himself inside to examine Vanessa's bloated body, and to officially pronounce her dead. Moments later he jumped out of the ambulance looking for Billy. He walked over to him with a depressing and yet scared look on his face.

"What's the cause Doc?" Billy asked presuming it was murder.

"Her eyes, it's strange, they're missing from her sockets," the coroner said from of the side of his mouth. He took the soggy cigar out and held it between his fingers as he spit the excess saliva to the road. He stuck the cigar back in his mouth and bit down feeling the wetness ooze onto his tongue.

Billy's eyes widened, and the first thing he thought of was the Dark Mountain Phantom. He quickly trotted over to the ambulance, and jumped in and carefully pulled her eyelids up. He saw the hollow sockets cleaned from the running river, and saw the familiar small marks on the bottom of her eyelids he's seen on his friend Lou, and Michelle.

He vaguely remembered she was one of the kids twenty five years ago who went up the mountain that crazy day. He jumped out of the ambulance, went over to the officers he was talking to, and explained to them he doesn't think the doctor did it, but he's still not ruling out murder.

He told them it could have been the Phantom. Some of the younger officers looked at him like he was cracking up, and as for the other two that's been on the force since Billy was a rookie, they knew exactly what he was talking about.

Billy walked to his car and called the dispatcher. He asked if she could call Jessica Michael's place to see if they were home, and for her to stay there until he arrived.

"Larry, I'm giving you the responsibility to tell Dr. Metagaham his ex-wife is dead," Billy shouted to him. "Don't forget to ask him some questions. Maybe he knows something."

"Yes Sir. I'll take care of it," he told him.

The coroner was still dumbfounded about the Vanessa's eyes, thinking and wondering what happened to her eyes. He'd been with the Glencliff Town for thirteen years, and he's never seen anything like this. He kept asking himself, "Why would someone gouge that woman's eyes out after they killed her? Or, did they dig her eyes out before they killed her?" As for Billy and the rest of the older townies, it was just all too familiar and something they'd want to forget.

11

"Did you say something?" Paul asked.

Shauna looked at him staring out the passenger window of her car. "No, did you hear me say something?" she asked in return.

"I thought I heard you call my name."

"No, I didn't say anything."

Paul looked out the window while they drove toward home, and kept his thoughts to himself. He felt he was getting extremely tired from running around and needed a little shut eye.

"There it is again, I heard someone say my name," he told her.

Shauna quickly looked at him, and then slowly looked back at the road.
She remembered the Phantom calling her name just before he showed up. She looked around the road but didn't see the Phantom anywhere, not even a shadow.

Paul continued to look out the window, as he put his ears to work and listened for anything, and everything. Suddenly, he heard his name whisper louder through the car. He quickly turned his head to the back seat and saw a faint dark shadow moving across the rear of the car. He closed his eyes and quickly opened them to focus better, and thought maybe he was just seeing things. Shauna slowly looked over at him again, and knew he was still hearing the Phantom calling his name.

She slammed her foot on the gas as the car flew down the road.
Paul glanced over and noticed the speedometer was reaching 85 miles an hour. He got frightened and gripped his hand on the door handle. "Christ, what the hell are you doing?" he shouted.

Shauna quickly slammed on the brakes and slid the car to a halt as Paul's hands slammed against the dashboard holding him self from going through the windshield.

"The Phantom is calling your name," she told him. "I'm trying to get away from him."
Suddenly they both looked out through the windshield. They saw the Phantom floating in front of the car and moving closer and closer

"I want my eyes!" the Phantom whispered loudly.

Paul and Shauna quickly jumped out and started running back down the street as fast as they could. Paul looked back and saw the Phantom was gone. He stopped running and called for Shauna to stop. Shauna looked back at Paul and saw the Phantom standing right next to him.

"Paul! Run!" she screamed. "He's right next to you!"

Paul sprinted down the street passing Shauna and didn't stop, nor did he even look back.

"Paul! Wait for me!" Shauna shouted, and suddenly felt a cold sensation on the back of her neck.

She watched Paul still running non-stop and knew the Phantom was behind her. She slowly turned around and saw the Phantom floating there. She watched him take the hood off his head and felt her body freeze up as she looked at him.

"Where are my eyes," the Phantom said softly.

Paul looked back and saw Shauna standing there in front of the Phantom, and stopped running. "Shauna!" he called out her name.

Shauna didn't respond, she couldn't, she felt the Phantom was trying to suck the life out of her, and then saw his boney fingers slowly emerge from his black shroud. She watched as the Phantom brought his fingers closer to her eyes.

"I want my eyes." the Phantom whispered.

Suddenly Paul tackled Shauna and threw her to the ground. The Phantom became enraged and screaming as he grabbed Paul by the back of the neck picking him up like a feather.

He threw him over the guard railing and down the hill. Paul clumsily fell and rolled down slamming against a big tree, and gashing the side of his arm. Ignoring the pain he quickly jumped to his feet, and scurried up the hill to save Shauna. He saw the Phantom leaning over her with his long boney fingers resting against her cheeks. He jumped the guard rail, and sprinted over to her. He grabbed her arm, and quickly dragged her away from the Phantom toward the car. He heard the Phantom scream again with anger

Suddenly he felt the Phantom's cold fingers wrap around his thin neck as the pressure from his strength crushed against his throat. Paul struggled to breathe as he still dragged Shauna to the car. He heard the Phantom scream louder than before as it sent chills up his spine. He knew the Phantom was angry as ever, but he didn't care. All he cared about was saving Shauna from getting killed

Paul felt his arms and his legs tingling from the lack of air. He slowly lost the strength in his grip and let Shauna go as he fell to the ground. The Phantom's hand still crushed against his throat as Paul struggled to breathe. Paul and the Phantom looked at each other face to face. Paul looked out the corner of his eye and saw Shauna slowly coming to. He felt the Phantom's cold blood drip on his face.

"I want my eyes!" the Phantom shouted, as his voice carried across the region.

Paul felt the cold feeling of the Phantom's finger press against his cheek, and with one quick push, the Phantom stuck his boney finger underneath and inside Paul's left eye. Paul screamed in pain as the Phantom slowly plucked his eyeball out from his socket. Shauna heard Paul's screaming and jumped up from the ground. She saw Paul squirming around with his hand pressed against his eye, and the blood drooling down his cheek. She looked at the Phantom's fingers with Paul's bloody eyeball. She screamed in hysterics as she stared at Paul's eye. She panicked and grabbed Paul's hand. She tried to drag him to the car as the Phantom held him down. She pulled and pulled but Paul wouldn't budge the Phantom's tight hold.

Suddenly the Phantom screamed louder than ever, and threw Paul's eye to the ground realizing it wasn't his. He grabbed Shauna by the front of her shirt, and slowly pulled her close to him. Paul dragged himself away, got to his feet, and tried to feel his way to the car. Shauna struggled and ripped her shirt off and ran toward Paul walking down the street with his hand out, and his other hand was covering his throbbing empty socket. She grabbed him and quickly pulled him to the car. The Phantom screamed again as his voice echoed across the region.

Shauna pushed Paul into the car and dove over him to the driver's side. Paul still screamed in pain as Shauna spun the tires up the road passing the Phantom still screaming with rage. She drove as fast as she could down the road and slid into the hospital's parking lot. She screamed for help for everyone to hear.

She screamed again for help, and opened the passenger door for Paul.

Two doctors came running out and looked at Paul's bloody face. A nurse came running out with a wheel chair as the doctor's threw him in the chair and wheeled him inside. Shauna's face was covered with black mascara that ran down her face from her tears. She looked at the nurse following the doctors and Paul inside and realized she was standing there with nothing but a skinny little white bra on. She crossed her arms and then saw the same nurse walk back holding an old white shirt she got from the lost and found. She smiled at her and grabbed the wrinkled shirt from her hand and threw it on. She slowly walked with the nurse shaking, and thinking about the entire trauma she and Paul just went through. When, just as she walked inside, she heard the same loud scream from the Phantom still echoing over the trees.

She stopped and looked up at the sky and wondered if the Phantom was getting more impatient for his eyes, or is he looking to kill everyone for just because. "Is something wrong?" the nurse asked watching Shauna stare up at the trees.

Shauna looked at her with a fake smile, and knew she didn't hear the Phantom screaming.

"Nothing," she replied as she tried to get the horror out of her mind, and walked into the hospital. Suddenly it dawned on her that Paul's mother was still in the hospital sitting outside of Stephanie's room.

12

Stephanie awoke from her near death sleep. Her mouth was dry and the skin on her fingers was tight. She remembered the dream she had with the rope around her neck and how Mitchell was killed by the Dark Mountain Phantom. She put her hand on her throat and felt the burn marks from the rope on both side of her neck. The thoughts went through her mind of how such a dream could be so incredibly real. She wondered since the marks on her neck felt real, did Mitchell really get killed from the Phantom? She pushed the button next to her bed as the nurse promptly walked in.

"Nurse, where did I get these marks on my neck?" she asked.

The nurse looked at her neck for a moment, and knew they weren't there yesterday.

"Let me get the doctor for you," she told her and walked out the door.

Stephanie just laid there as the nurse walked down the hall looking for her doctor with the same question on her mind as well, since the open wound wasn't even covered up, and she knew for a fact it wasn't there at all yesterday

The doctor strolled into her room and grabbed the clip board hanging off the side of the bed. He stared at the board for a moment, looked at her and her bandages wrapped around her head. "For a pretty girl she looks awful," he thought to himself.

"Let me take a look at these marks you're complaining about," he told her and put his fingers near the area. He noticed they were extremely fresh and still somewhat bleeding. He glanced at her clipboard again, and saw that she was checked in four days ago from a car accident. He looked at the burns again with a puzzling look on his face.

"Nurse, get some Neosporin, and some gauze. We need to stop this from getting more infected," he said as he squeezed some of the infection out with his fingers and saw Stephanie bite down on the bottom of her lip.

"More infected?" Stephanie asked.

"Yes, it's a little infected. That's why you're feeling a little pain."

"These marks are from the accident?"

"Yes, it looks to be from the accident," He spit out a lie through his teeth. "You'll be fine in a little while. I'll come back soon and check up on you later." He walked out of the room as the nurse sat down next to Stephanie, and moved her head to one side to cover up the burn mark. The doctor walked down the hall wondering why he didn't see the burn marks before.

Stephanie closed her eyes for a brief moment and thought about Mitchell. She wondered if he would ever change, and thought maybe she would start dating him sometime again in the near future. She thought about his smile and his affectionate ways, and how he made her feel safe when they were together.

She started to doze off when Paul's mother quietly walked in and sat down on her bed smiling at her. Stephanie opened her eyes and smiled back when unexpectedly Shauna walked in crying and ran over and gave Paul's mother a big hug, and started telling her the story of what happened. Paul's mother started to cry and quickly bolted out of the room and down the hallway. Shauna watched Paul's mother run down the hall as fast as she could as the fear and her thoughts of the worst went through her mind. She glanced back over at Stephanie crying as well. She looked at her and didn't remember seeing the bandages wrapped around her neck the last time she visited. She walked over and sat down on her bed. "Is it true?" Stephanie asked.

"Is what true?"

"Mitchell, he's dead isn't he. I saw him in my dreams. The Phantom killed him."

Shauna started to cry harder and shook her head yes. Stephanie rolled over to one side letting the tears run down to the pillow, and to hide her emotions.

"Steph, I'm sorry. We wanted to tell you, but the doctor said we should wait until you were feeling better."

"When, when did he die?" she asked softly.

"He died the same day you crashed your car. His neck was broken and his eyes were taken from him."

"Who killed him?" She asked remembering her dream about the evil Phantom, but what she really wanted was to hear it in Shauna's words.

"The Dark Mountain Phantom did it," Shauna told her.

Silence fell over the room as Shauna thought about Paul and his mother in the emergency room. She saw Stephanie slowly sit up and looked at her directly in the eyes. She watched her as she took the pins out of her head bandage, and unraveled it until it was completely off.

"What does it look like?" Stephanie asked.

Shauna stared at the cuts and bruises all over her forehead. The first thing Shauna thought was Stephanie was lucky to be alive. She saw the cut on her forehead and counted the six stitches that tied her skin together. "They shaved some of your hair off," she told her.

"What else do you see?" Stephanie asked demandingly.

"Shauna was not going to tell her she looked awful. She didn't want to tell her anything. She smiled at Stephanie, and reached over and gave her best friend a soft kiss on the lips.

"Stephanie I love you very much. You're my best friend and you need your rest. I'm going to see how Paul is doing okay. I'll be back real soon," she told her and walked out of the room without saying anything else. She didn't have to.

Stephanie knew she looked terrible. She also knew Shauna wanted to go cry somewhere alone, as she watched her turn the corner.

Shauna walked toward the elevator when the tears started to flow. She quickly ducked into an empty dark room and curled up to a ball on a cold bed. She let it all out and nothing was stopping her from crying. All the pain, fear, worry, and emotional torture that built up finally had come to a head. She laid there crying harder than she's ever cried before, and wanting it all to go away. She thought of the little hiking adventure they had up the mountain, and wished it never even happened. Mitchell was dead, and as far as she's concerned it was for the better. But she wasn't going to tell anybody that, especially not Stephanie. Stephanie, who she's loved like a sister for all these years almost died, and for some reason, in some weird way she felt like she did. She straightened herself out on the bed, and took a deep breath trying to regain control of her emotions. It was hard but she wanted to show everyone she was the strong one, even though deep down she knew she was the most emotional of anyone. She laid there still thinking of everything and everybody. Paul had lost an eye, the evil Phantom was still on the loose, and didn't have a clue of how to stop it.

She remembered her and her friends taking the emeralds, and then remembered Mitchell acting like a total ass when he held them in his hands. She sat up on the bed still thinking about the stones. "Mmm," she thought to herself. "If I were Mitchell, where would I have put the emeralds?" Suddenly, she felt so, not alone. She quickly looked around the room in the darkness but didn't see anyone. She felt a cold sense in the air. Panic instantly absorbed her body as she started to shake uncontrollably.

"I don't have your eyes!" she shouted at the top of her voice thinking it was the Phantom in the room.

The lights quickly went on. "What the hell are you doing in here!" shouted the Heavy black nurse.

"I asked you a question!" shouted the nurse again. "What are you doing in here?"

"N-Nothing ma'am, I was just..."

"You were just what? Get your ass out of this room before I call security. You know better than to contaminate a sterile room!"

Shauna walked toward the door and squeezed by the heavy nurse as she felt her eyes burning with anger. "I'm sorry. I didn't…"

"Don't bother, just get out!"

Shauna hurriedly walked down the hall wiping her eyes, and trying not to show any signs of a breakdown. She jumped on the elevator and looked one last time at the heavy nurse still staring at her with anger until the door slid closed. She walked off the elevator and walked to the emergency room where she saw Paul's mother with her arms crossed and the police chief standing there. She walked over and gave Paul's mother a big hug.

"Is he gonna be okay?" Shauna asked.

"He's in surgery right now. The doctor's seem to think he was stuck in the eye with a stick of some sort," Paul's mother replied.

"Did you see what happened?" The chief asked.

"Yes, I did," Shauna said nervously. "I saw the Dark Mountain Phantom holding Paul's eye stuck to his finger."

Chills went up everyone's spine as Shauna looked at Paul's mother and the chief staring at each other. They knew Paul was lucky, but the next time he wouldn't be.

"What are we going to do?" Shauna asked. "The Phantom is everywhere."

The chief looked at Shauna for a moment, and thought to himself. "We need to find the emeralds, and we need to find them fast," he told them.

Paul's mother needed a hug so she put her arms around the chief and held him tight. The chief felt her soft body against him, and unnoticeably smiled when he smelt her perfume linger to his nose. He closed his eyes and imagined being in her arms forever.

"Billy what are we going to do?" Paul's mother asked as she squeezed him tighter, and heard Sheila's voice through his radio.

"Yeah, go ahead," he replied with a strong voice pulling away from Paul's mother. "There's another body found near Woodland Bridge. The woman is still there who made the call."

"I'm on my way," he quickly headed out of the hospital and jumped into his police cruiser.

The doctor came out, slipped his glasses off his nose and walked over to Paul's mother. "Mrs. Michael's?" the doctor said.

"Yes," she replied and started to shake fearing the worst.

"Let's have a seat."

"Is it bad?" She started to think more of the worst.

"Your son, he's a remarkable boy."

"Yes I know doctor, is he going to be alright?" She insisted he get to the point.

"Paul is going to be fine. He's going to need to get fitted for a glass eye when his body heals the wounds."

Paul's mother took a deep breath and grabbed Shauna's hand. "Can I go see him?"

"He's being taking to I.C.U. when he wakes up you can see him then."

"When do you think he'll wake up?" she asked.

"He should be awake within the next three to four hours."

Paul's mother stood up and walked around for a moment thinking and worrying. She wondered if his life will be as normal as it always has been, or is he going to sink into depression.

The chief drove up to the bridge and saw the ambulance, and his police officers looking down at the dead body. He looked over and saw that this time, the body was facing up. He looked down at the body hard hoping it was not another Phantom attack.

"Hey Chief," Scotty shouted from the body. "It's the old man that lives near the railroad bridge up river!"

"Does he still have his eyes!" the chief shouted back.

He watched as Scotty pulled his eyelids open, turned the dead man's head to the right, and then to the left.

"Yeah!" Scotty shouted. "He looks like he just died and fell into the water!"

"Bring him up!" the chief said with a sigh of relief.

"He still has his fishing rod in his hand!" Scotty yelled. "It's a nice one. Chief can I have it!" He asked as everyone started to laugh.

"Sure, whatever Scotty," The chief said and started to laugh along with the others. The chief watched as the paramedics dragged the old man up on the stretcher, when he felt a tapping on his shoulder.

"I'm the one who found the man floating in the water," the woman said.

The chief looked at her, and thought she looked scared and alone. "I didn't know what to do, so I waved a passing car down and they called the police," she told him.

"Where is the car now ma'am?"

"He left."

"Did he see the body?"

"No, he just called the police, and said there was a body in the water."

"Did you already give a statement to someone?"

"Yes."

"Do you need a ride home, or do you have a car?"

"I could use a lift home."

"Where do you live?"

"I live in the center of town."

"Okay, I'll give you a ride in a little bit. Just have a seat on the guard rail, and we'll leave in a short while."

"Okay."

After three or so hours Paul's mother was still pacing the floor, when a nurse came over and told her Paul had just woken up and she could go see him. She hurriedly walked down the hallway, and walked into his room and saw the white bandage across his eye. He still was somewhat incoherent of what was happening, but he did manage to focus on his mother.

"Mom," he said softly. "I'm sorry. I don't know what happened," He started to tear from his good eye. His mother put her arms around him and started to cry herself.

"It's okay Paul, you didn't do anything," she told him.

"The Phantom pulled my eye out."

"Shh Paul, everything is going to be okay, shh."

"Shauna, is she here with you?"

"Shauna is here. She's not going anywhere.

13

Billy drove away from Woodland Bridge after they fished the old man out of the river, and loaded him into the meat wagon. He looked over at the woman with long blonde hair, and blue eyes. She wore a black mini skirt that seemed even shorter against the length of her long thin legs, and matched her tight shirt that showed the essence of an attractive woman. Billy realized he's never seen this beautiful woman before as he kept admiring her model figure while he drove slowly down the road toward the center of town. The woman sat quietly looking out the window, nervous, and thinking of her own personal thoughts until she got home.

"Did you just move here Miss?" Billy asked and stuck a straw from his old ice coffee in his mouth. He chewed on the end for a moment and waited for her to answer him.

"I said did you just move here Miss?" He asked again, but she still looked out the window as Billy thought she was ignoring him.

He reached over and touched the woman on her arm, as the woman quickly snapped her arm away and looked at him. She glared at him thinking he was coming on to her

"I said did you just move here?" He shouted and noticed the woman was reading his lips.

"Yes, I moved from Twin Mountains with my boyfriend," she said and cracked a fake smile.

Billy quickly glanced over at her ear and saw a small hearing aid just a little covered from her hair.

"We didn't like the place we were living at so we moved here," she told him.

"It's a nice town," He said looking at her. "It's quiet. Why were you at Woodland Bridge?" he asked.

"I was walking home from having lunch with my boyfriend," she told him.

Billy looked at her still chewing on the end of the straw with an unnoticeable smile, and wondered if she was telling the truth, or was she just covering her tracks, but he was just using his police-trained mind since he thought everyone was guilty until proven innocent.

"What's your name?" he asked, as he looked down at her long thin legs again.

"Allison," she said closing her legs tight noticing he was staring.

"We're almost at the center of town. Where do you live?" he glanced back at the road.

"I live over the hardware store. You can drop me off at the end of the parking lot."

Billy pulled up to the front door of the hardware store and stopped. Allison smiled at him, opened the door, and slid both legs out at the same time. Billy chewed hard down on the straw, and watched her standup as he checked out her back side.

"Thank you officer, I appreciate it. Thank you," she politely told him and walked toward the side of the building.

Billy watched her until she turned the corner. He rolled down his window, threw out the chewed straw, and thought about Jessica Michaels and wondered if she would look good in a mini skirt. "Some guys have all the luck." He said out loud. He looked out the passenger side window and watched Allison walking up the stairs. "God damn!" he said, as he drove off.

He drove down the street remembering Shauna telling him the Phantom is everywhere. He quickly got on the radio and called out to Sheila.

"Yes Chief, I'm here," Sheila answered through the radio.

"I'm heading over to the Lacroix's, and see if I can talk to them about some issues that just came up."

"Receive."

"I shouldn't be too long."

Billy drove up to the house, and stepped out of the car. He could feel the sense of death in the air and started to remember the time when his best friend Lou was killed. He walked up the sidewalk as Mitchell's mother opened the door with Mitchell's much older sister Alyssa behind her.

"Hello Mrs. Lacroix, how are you?" Billy asked being polite.

"Hello Billy, is there something I can help you with?"

"Mom, Let him in," Alyssa spoke out.

Mitchell's mother stepped back, and let Billy enter. He took his hat off and looked around the house. He saw what's left of the grandparents quietly sitting in the living room, and Mitchell's father slouched down in the chair with his head down. Billy could still sense the death in the air and stared at Mitchell's father for a moment. He could tell he felt like there was nothing left to live for, and he's already died inside.

"Mrs. Lacroix, may I take a look around Mitchell's room for a moment? I need to see if I can find anything that would relate to his death," he asked her.

Mitchell's mother without saying a word, pointed her finger up the stairs, and walked into the living room.

"I'll show him his room," Alyssa said as she stepped up on the first step and looked back at Billy. Unconsciously she looked down at his ring finger, and noticed he wasn't wearing a wedding band.

Billy walked behind Alyssa up the stairs watching every sexy step she took. He remembered her from the time he went to the haunted house with his friends; the same night they released the first Friday the 13th movie. He saw her inside the haunted house, and remembered her falling into his arms when she got scared.

They were still just kids then, but he also remembered her beautiful soft eyes sparkling in the flashing light, and her warm huggable body against his. "She's still too high class for me. But damn she still looks good," he thought.

He walked up the hardwood floor stairs and clanked his boots down the hall trying to clear his mind of his memories of her, and stopped in front of Mitchell's room. He looked at the posters of beautiful models half dressed on the wall, and saw his collection of Star Trek plates on the bureau. Alyssa stood in front of the door fixing her black mini dress, and ignored Mitchell's room like he never existed.

Billy was still looking around in every direction, when he saw Alyssa bend down and play with her shoes. He rolled his eyes with a smile, and tried not to look at her exposing cleavage.

He looked down to the floor and saw Mitchell's backpack leaning against his bed. He picked it up and looked inside. "Damn," he said to himself and threw the backpack back on the floor when suddenly he heard a loud thud. He slowly picked up the backpack again, and saw one of the green shining emeralds lying on the floor. He picked it up and smiled as he found what he was looking for.

"Where's the other one?" he asked himself.

Alyssa walked in the room and looked at the emerald in his hand.

"What is that?" she asked, with her eyes admiring the beauty.

"This is why Mitchell was killed," he told her. "But where is the other one?"

"Billy, I didn't even know he had them. I don't even know what that is."

"I know you don't. But we need to find the other one." Billy picked up the backpack and checked all of the pockets and sleeves, but no emerald. He stuck his hand in each pocket again, and then pushed against the last pocket. His fingers went through the bottom and figured he must have dropped it somewhere when he was using his backpack.

"When was the last time Mitchell used this backpack?" he asked.

Alyssa looked at him and shrugged her shoulders. "I have no idea, maybe you should ask Mom," she told him and crossed her arms.

"I need to go," he told her and swiftly walked out of the room.

Billy stomped down the stairs when he looked over and saw Mitchell's mother on the phone. He waited until she was off, when surprisingly enough, she handed him the phone.

"Hello," he said confused.

"Billy, this is Jessica."

"Hi Jess. How did you know I was here?"

"Sheila told me."

"Oh, well, what's on your mind?"

"Paul's gone back into surgery. His eye wound hasn't stopped bleeding."

"Jess, I found one of the emeralds."

Silence fell over the phone when he said those words to her. "Jess, are you there?"

"Yes, I'm here. Where's the other one?" she asked.

"I don't know."

"Billy, I really could use a hug from you right now," she told him.

Billy stood there somewhat in shock. He wanted to run down to the hospital and hold her for as long as he could, but he knew he needed to do his job.

"I'll come over as soon as I can figure out where the other stone is," he said to her.

"Okay…. But I hope to see you real soon."

"Okay hon—okay Jess, I'll see you soon." He hung up the phone realizing he almost called her honey, and then chuckled a bit.

"Honey," Alyssa said from the bottom step. "You almost called Jessica Michaels 'honey'. Are you seeing that woman?" she asked with an attitude.

"No, and even if I was, it's none of your business," Billy snapped and glared at her and swung open the door. "Once a bitch, always a bitch," he thought to himself. "No wonder why she's still single."

Alyssa crossed her arms and watched him walk down the sidewalk, and glanced over at her aging parents. She wondered if they're ever going to put this tragic nightmare past them, or are they going to be in mourning until their own passing. She thought of Mitchell and how she never really got to be a big sister to him since she was already out of high school, and moved out to college when he was born. Sort of a mid life crisis mistake if you put it in black and white. She looked back one more time at Billy driving down the street, and walked into the living room and sat down on the couch joining her family in watching the television in silence.

14

Stephanie listened to the doctor telling her about the healing process she's going to go through in the weeks ahead. She listened to him with her father sitting next to her, and unconsciously started thinking about Mitchell. She wanted to forgive him for being such an asshole, and get a big hug from him. But she knew he was dead, and she'll never see him again. She started to weep as her father put his arm around her, and held her close.

Shauna walked into the room as Stephanie turned her head toward the window and tried to hide her tears, and wiped them off with the bed sheet. Her father stood up and gave Shauna a hug to console her about Paul's accident.

"What accident?" Stephanie shouted.

Shauna looked at her with her exhausted eyes. She hadn't slept in two days, and her eyes had dark bags under them and she somewhat swayed while standing.

"Paul lost his left eye," Shauna told her.

"How did he loose an eye?"

Shauna paused for a moment and thought about the horror her, and Paul went through.

"The Phantom took it," she whispered as she started to tear.

"Stephanie, I think you're well enough to go home, and have your father take care of you," The doctor spoke up. "But just bear in mind, you're still going to have a lot of head aches for a while."

"Okay doctor," Stephanie agreed.

Stephanie's father shook hands with the doctor, and talked a bit with him quietly.

Shauna reached over and hugged her best friend tight. She still wanted all the nightmares to go away.

"Is Paul going to be alright?" Stephanie asked.

"He'll be fine, but we need to find the emeralds Mitchell took from the rocks."

Suddenly, the doctor and Stephanie's father stopped talking, and looked over at Shauna. Shauna glanced over feeling their eyes burning into her.

"What?" she asked.

"What are you talking about?" Stephanie's father asked.

"Nothing, you wouldn't understand," she told him.

"Shauna, I do understand. You're talking about the worst nightmare of all time."

"That explains why the dead boy came here a few days back without his eyes. The Phantom, he's awake," the doctor exclaimed punching his left palm with a fist.

"Mitchell," Stephanie's father said.

"Yes, that name is correct. Mitchell Lacroix."

"How do you know about the Phantom?" Shauna asked.

"I lived through the horror years ago." Stephanie's father walked over and looked out the window. He remembered everything for a brief moment. "My brother Lou was killed by the Phantom."

Stephanie nudged Shauna to get off the bed, and slid her feet over and onto the floor.

"Stephanie, what are you doing?" her father asked.

"Let her do what she wants," The doctor said and grabbed his arm to stay where he was.

Everyone watched as Stephanie stood up on the cold floor, and smiled trying to hide the pain. She put her hand out reaching for something to hold as Shauna quickly let her grab her arm for balance.

Shauna smiled joyfully when Stephanie was standing on her own. "Let's take you home Steph," Shauna said putting her arm around her waist, and kissed her on the cheek.

15

Paul's mother sat in the emergency room waiting for more results from the doctor, when the chief walked up behind her, and affectionately put his hand on her shoulder. Paul's mother jumped out of her seat, put her arms around him and squeezed him tight.

"I found one of the emeralds," he told her sparking the conversation again.

"I know you told me on the phone," she said. "But where did you find it?"

"I found it in Mitchell's backpack. But like I said, I only found one."

"Where do you think the other one could be? Do you think maybe someone else has it?"

"That's why I'm here. I was told Stephanie is visiting Shauna right now."

"Yes she is. She's upstairs with her."

"I need to go pay a visit. By the way how's Paul doing?" he asked giving her a quick affectionate hug.

"He's still in surgery, but I haven't heard a word for more than three hours."

"He'll be fine, I have a gut feeling," he commented hoping she'll feel better with those words

Billy walked down the hall, pushed open the doors and looked back at her with a smile.

"They're in room 106!" she shouted before the doors swung closed.

"Hello," Billy said knocking on the door, and saw Stephanie just about ready to leave the hospital.

"Hello Chief, is there something we can do for you?" Stephanie's father asked.

"Yes, I need to ask Stephanie and her friend Shauna some questions if you don't mind."

"Not at all," he told him.

Billy sat down on the chair next to Stephanie's bed, and noticed Shauna had a lot of scrapes and bruises on her face and arms.

"Can you tell me about the emeralds?" he asked.

Shauna looked at Stephanie trying to avoid the question, but she knew someday it was going to be inevitable, and she would have to tell all.

"We got them when we went hiking up on the mountain," Stephanie told him.

Her father walked over and sat down next to her on the bed.

"Where exactly did you get the emeralds?" Billy asked already knowing where the emeralds were

"Inside some rocks," Shauna said. "Didn't we go over this at the Michael's house?" she asked thoughtlessly.

"Who opened the rocks?" Billy asked ignoring her bitchy attitude, and proceeded to keep asking the questions.

"Paul did," Stephanie said and looked over at the doctor with his arms crossed. The doctor knew what they were talking about, and yet, he didn't want to get involved, so he put Stephanie's clip board down, and quickly walked out of the room giving the chief a dirty look.

Silence fell in the room for a moment when the doctor left, as Billy stood up and walked over to the window staring down at the parking lot.

"Where's the other emerald?" he snipped with a slight attitude.

Shauna looked over at him with confusion. "Mitchell had both of them," she snapped back at him.

Billy quickly turned around and glared at her. He pulled out the emerald he had in his pocket and tossed it on the bed, and went back and sat down in the chair.

"There was only one in his backpack. Where's the other one, Shauna!" he shouted hoping she would back down.

Stephanie reached over, and grabbed the emerald. She looked at it and remembered standing outside the rocks. Suddenly the emerald started to glow as she felt her fingers getting warm. She tossed it back on the bed, as they all stared at the glowing stone.

"Where's the other stone?" Billy asked, and crossed his arms waiting for an answer.

"We don't know where the other one is. Mitchell had both of them the whole time," Stephanie pleaded.

"Yeah, the jerk wouldn't let anyone else get close to them," Shauna told him.

"More people are going to die if we don't find the other stone. So I need your help."

"Chief, what do you want us to do?" Stephanie asked and felt her father's arm wrap around her shoulders. "Dad," Stephanie snapped. "I don't want to be touched," She pushed his arm away.

They all looked at each other in silence, thinking, and wondering where the other stone could be. Billy stood up off the chair, picked the stone up off the bed, and put it back in his pocket.

"Call me when you're ready to tell me where the other stone is. In the mean time, everyone you know will be dieing soon," he told them and walked out of the room.

"Let's take you home now," Stephanie's father said.

Billy walked back down to the emergency room, frustrated to the limit since he got nowhere with the girls, and saw Jessica still sitting and reading an outdated magazine. He put his hand on her shoulder, and squeezed with a little affection. "How's Paul doing?" he asked.

"He's out of surgery now, but I have to wait until the doctor says I can go see him again."

"Jess, why don't you go home and get some rest. He'll be fine."

"No, I can't. What if he wakes up and I'm not here."

"He'll be fine. Let me take you home, and in a couple of hours I'll bring you back."

She threw the magazine on the table and got up from the chair and grabbed his hand. She put her arm around him and hugged him.

"What happened with Shauna? Did you find out where the other stone is?" she asked.

"No, they wouldn't tell me, or they didn't know. I think they know but they're too scared to tell."

"The Phantom is gonna kill everyone and anyone until he finds both of them."

"I know, I told them that."

"What about that old man that sits on the park bench in front of the little store?"

"Jess, if I recall, right now you're the only one who can see him."

"Yeah, but he also told me he sees things. Maybe he can tell us where the stone is."

"Let's go see him, or should I say, let's have you go see him."

Paul's mother grabbed her purse and walked out of the hospital still holding onto Billy's hand as she walked with him to the cruiser. Billy the gentleman he is opened the passenger door for her. Unsurprisingly, Paul's mother turned around and kissed Billy on the lips. She sat in the car holding a smile as Billy shut the door knowing that she felt the same way about him.

Billy drove down Main Street looking at every park bench hoping to see the old man.
"Is that him?" Billy asked.

"No, he's an old man with black sun glasses on. There he is, stop the car."

Billy stopped the car as Paul's mother jumped out and stared at the old man. He sat on the bench with a smile, and slightly leaned against his cane with both hands on the handle.

"After all these years he still looks the same," she thought to herself. She walked across the street, as Billy looked on through the window of the cruiser hoping he could see who, or where he was.

She walked up to the old man, and quickly glanced back at Billy, and then looked back at the old man. "What do you see old man?" she asked hesitantly.

The old man kept smiling and didn't say a word.

"I said what do you see?"

"Are you alright Jessica?" a woman asked coming out of the card shop. The woman looked at her confused and wondered if she needed psychological help, then waved her arm high in the air to say hi to Billy.

"Yes, I'm fine Sue. How are you today?" she asked feeling a little embarrassed.

"I'm fine. I'm on my way to the church memorial for Mitchell Lacroix. Are you going?"

"I'll be there in a little while." She looked at the way Sue was dressed, and thought her black mini skirt with a slit high up the front. Black high boots that wrapped around her thin legs and her black shoulder less tight shirt protruding her nipples she was wearing was a little to risque for a church memorial.

"It's a shame what happened to him. He was such a nice boy," Sue commented, and didn't dare to tell Jessica she had a little sexual affair with Mitchell two months before when her and her husband willingly split up.

Mitchell had come wandering over one hot afternoon to trim the hedges. Jessica knew something was going on when she realized Mitchell was over her house everyday after school, as she said to trim the hedges. No kids, no dogs, not even a fish tank, and yet the hedges, well, they were only five feet long across the side of the house. Mitchell once said. "A little trim is good; you can always see what you're playing with."

"I need to run. I hope to see you at the memorial," Sue walked down the sidewalk to her convertible Plymouth Sundance. Sue waved one more time at Billy before she jumped into her car.

"Such a slut," she said in a low tone of voice. "No wonder why her husband left her." She looked back down at the park bench, and saw the old man still sitting there smiling and holding his cane. She noticed a peculiar look about him, like he was looking at her, or through her.

"You said to me before that you see things," she told him. "I want to know if you see anything. Where is the other stone?" she asked demandingly.

The old man turned his head and just smiled.

Jessica got impatient with just his ongoing smile and decided it was a waste of time to be talking to someone who doesn't even exist, and walked toward the cruiser.

"The stone is in the middle of the dark forest!" the man shouted at her. "That's where you'll find it. But remember, the Phantom is watching you. He knows who you are."

Jessica stopped in the middle of the road, and turned around. She walked back to the old man, and waited for him to tell her more.

"The emerald fell out of the boy's bag, and landed on the ground near the wolf's food," He said. "Be careful of the hanging ropes, they bite."

"What ropes?" she asked wondering.

The old man smiled as he slowly faded away. Jessica watched as he disappeared into thin air. She walked back to the car and sat down in the passenger seat. She sighed, and waved her hand in silence for Billy to drive off.

"Well," Billy said waiting for an explanation.

"Just drive for a little while," she told him out of frustration.

Silence fell in the car for a short while until they drove by the broken guard rail where Stephanie crashed through. Jessica looked at the trail she made with her car, and thought she saw someone, or something run behind the tree Stephanie hit with her car.

"Wait!" she shouted, as Billy slammed his foot on the brake and the car quickly came to a screeching stop. "I saw someone go behind the tree down there." She pointed her finger toward the river's edge.

Billy quickly got out. He looked around down near the river's edge. He didn't see anything but Stephanie's old tire marks in the grass. Jessica jumped out and slid down the hill, and looked around the tree. She too, didn't see anything, or anyone.

Billy slid down the tire trail and caught up with her looking up at the bridge, when suddenly Billy and Jessica felt the air go strange, like it turned thin and bitter cold. Billy looked at Jessica and knew he'd felt this strangeness before.

"The Phantom is near," Billy whispered. They both could sense the Phantom being close by, and Jessica quickly became very scared to point of almost shaking. She remembers the Phantom twenty five years ago, and she never forgot the black hollow eyes staring down at her.

16

The funeral memorial was being held this morning at the old congregational church for Mitchell Lacroix on Main Street at 11 a.m. The church bell rang loud and echoed for the whole town to hear, as a group of teenage kids nearby looked up to see the church bell swinging. The music was playing very soft as the Reverend sat alone holding the Book of God near the gold-plated cross hanging in the middle of the paint chipped wall. Every family member and friend were coming almost at the same time, filling the parking lot and the side of the road with their automobiles.

History as it's written in the lobby of the old church, says that a worn out Black man who worked most of his life as a slave drifting for years came here looking for a place to feel free, and be free. One day he kneeled down in the middle of a tall grass field to pray for help, and finally to forgive the men who had killed his family the year President Lincoln freed his brothers and sisters. He looked up to the sky and raised his hands hoping God was listening, when unexpectedly heard the voice from above. "If you want to pray to me, you must build me a home."

He collected all the rocks he could find from a great distance in every direction, and built the house for God where it still stands today. Four months after the stone church was finished, the mayor's wife was found dead on her living room floor with a knife stabbed deeply into her chest. The farmer who lived next door was secretly in love with the mayor's wife became enraged, and said it was the lonely Black man who lives in the church just over the horizon.

Before he could prove his innocence to the angry mob, the men strung him up hanging him from the white-candled chandelier until he was dead, and then burned the roof off the church.

Many years after the brutal hanging, a small group of loyal parishioners collected pieces of the puzzle and proved the Black man's innocence, and rebuilt the church with more added features in honor of the his name and faith to the church. The one picture that was found buried under the dirt in front of the church, is hanging next to his biographical article in framed glass.

In memory of our first Reverend of the Congregational Church,

Samuel J. Williamson Jr.

Mitchell's parents and Alyssa were sitting in the front of the church, closest to the open casket with large bouquets of flowers tied with yellow and white ribbons from friends and neighbors that overwhelmed each end of his casket.

Alyssa sat next to her aging father who slumped himself down in the pew hiding away from the world with his head down, or perhaps afraid to see his only son stretched out in a box.

"Dad, sit up. You're making a fool of yourself," Alyssa whispered to him and carefully tugged against his arm.

Mitchell's mother ignored her husband and talked with everyone who came near. She wanted to hide the pain and the loss of her son, but she also wanted to break down in tears and ask for God to bring her son back.

The reverend stood up and walked over to the podium fixing his glasses, and paused for a moment until everyone sat down. He looked over at the elderly lady playing the piano to have her stop, and saw she had lifted her frail fingers off the keys

"For the sadness and loss of our beloved brother…." The reverend started to give his funeral homily, and constantly looked over at Mitchell's family. He noticed Alyssa was the only one who wasn't tearing or paying any attention to him at all. Instead she looked away toward the religious painted windows wondering how much comes light through, and thought about her last boyfriend and why he doesn't call her anymore.

"As we say our goodbyes to our beloved Mitchell…" He spoke loudly, and saw the police chief and Paul's mother unnoticeably walk in and sat down in the last pew.

Alyssa looked over and caught the Reverend's eyes staring out toward the back of the church. She twisted her head and glanced at them sitting down close to each other, and wondered if they were holding hands. She looked back at the Reverend still waving his hands as he continued with his speech.

Just then, Mitchell's father quietly put his head down. He took a long lasting deep breath, closed his eyes, and leaned his frail body up against Alyssa.

"Dad, get up," she whispered nudging him, and noticed he didn't respond.

"Dad," She said puzzled and put her hand on his chest.

"Dad!" she shouted and realized he wasn't breathing.

The Reverend stopped his speech, and hurriedly went over to Mitchell's father to see if he was okay.

"Dad!" she shouted louder as she panicked and got the crowds attention than some of the family's close friends hurriedly came over.

Billy jumped out of the pew and ran over turning his portable radio on. He touched his neck for a pulse, and felt his chest for his heart beat. He quickly called for an ambulance, and helped lie him down on the pew.

Alyssa knew her father had died the moment she felt him lean against her. She knew someday her father would pass on because of the heart complications he's had in the last five years. "But why now?" she asked herself.

Alyssa's mother sat next to her husband holding his hand and rubbing his face. She could feel the lifeless sensation on her fingers, mumbling to herself with tears ready to explode from her eyes.

Minutes went by as Paul's mother quietly sat alone watching from the back of the church, as the EMT's tried to revive Mitchell's father. She too was wondering why he had passed away on a time when his family needed him the most.

The chief looked back at Jessica slowly nodding, and gave her a look gesturing to her that he has indeed died.

Jessica put her head down in silence for a moment and started to pray for the family, when suddenly she noticed the church had become extremely quiet as the EMT's put him on the stretcher and covered him over with a white sheet.

The Reverend quoted his last testimony from the Bible, placed a small cross on Mr. Lacroix's chest, and gave his condolences to Mitchell's mother and sister. Mitchell's mother was crying on her next door neighbors shoulder, as Alyssa stood alone with her arms crossed and tears running down her face not knowing what to do next.

Paul's mother got up and decided to walk over to give her condolences, even though when they were in high school they never liked each other, or even spoke with a friendly voice, she still needed to do the right thing.

Alyssa saw her walking over to her, as she put her old evil thoughts behind her for the first time since high school, and finally accepted Jessica's condolences.

"Well, I guess we need to get ready for another funeral, don't we?" Alyssa said and wiped her eyes.

"Yes, I guess we do," they heard Mitchell's mother speak walking toward them. "He's wanted to die for a long time, and now since Mitchell's gone, he felt there wasn't anything left," she told them trying to accept his passing and as always, be the strong one in the family.

The chief listened to Mitchell's mother, and remembered thinking the same thing at their house just days ago.

Everyone watched as the EMT's wheeled Mitchell's father out of the church and into the coroner's wagon. Mitchell's mother slowly walked down the center aisle holding in her tears with Alyssa, and turned around one last time to see her son lying in the casket.

"Daddy's with you now son," she whispered and turned back toward the door.

The chief and Jessica stood next to each other wondering what happens at a time like this.

"Does the Reverend keep going with Mitchell's memorial? Or is it cancelled on account of another family member has died?"

"This has been one hell of a bad week," Paul's mother quietly said shaking her head.

"Yes it has. He was ready to die any ways," The chief replied.

Paul's mother sat down on the pew looking for the chief to sit down with her until the rest of the mourners left. She stared at Mitchell's casket, and remembered her best friend in a similar color, and she also remembered sitting in the same pew.

The chief walked away to go do his job as a police officer, and to give his own condolences to the family. He looked over at the Reverend and unexpectedly, he saw an old man standing behind him with dark sun glasses on smiling at him, and holding a cane. He walked toward the Reverend to talk to the man, when the elderly lady that played the piano caught him, and asked him why he didn't come to church except for when he only has to.

"Mrs. Needleson, I'm a very busy man, and these days I just don't have time every week," he told her trying to be nice. When he looked up to see the old man, he noticed he was gone. He looked around to find him somewhere walking away from the church, suddenly, and oddly enough, he felt very alone

"William, tell your mother I said hi. It's been a long time since we talked," Mrs. Needleson said patting her hand against his arm.

Billy looked down at her and paused for a moment. He remembered telling her every time they talked, that his mother had been dead for years.

"I'll tell her that you said hi Mrs. Needleson," he said and smiled at her.

"William," Mrs. Needleson said somewhat sternly and then pursed her lips, and obviously thinking of something serious to say. "I know you visit your mother every month. That's why I keep telling you to say 'hi' to your mother for me. You must realize your mother's memory lives on in many people in this town,"

"Yes I do Mrs. Needleson," Billy said somewhat choked up, because he was never comfortable talking about his mother since she's been dead these years. "Now, Mrs. Needleson, if there's anything else, I have some things I need to attend to,"

Mrs. Needleson grabbed his arm. Billy was somewhat stunned at this seemingly frail looking lady's grip. Her hand felt like a vise around Billy's wrist. "William," she whispered pulling him closer to talk in his ear. "The memories of that Phantom will forever live in this small town, and the word in the air says that he's on the hunt again. You know that…that thing up there stole my granddaddy's eyes right in front of me when I was ten years of age. Well William you can go now, I just wanted to tell you that, because I know what you and that Jessica Michael's girl are up to," Mrs. Needleson stared deep into Billy's eyes. "You just make sure who ever has those wretched jewels gives them back to the mountain," With that said, she let go of his arm, turned around and began to walk away with the slightest hint of a limp.

Billy watched her for a minute rubbing his wrist, and noticed that old lady had actually drawn a small dose of blood with her fingernails. "Son of a bitch," he said pulling a white handkerchief out of his pocket and wiped the blood.

Paul's mother exited the church and squint her eyes from the sun. She pulled out her sunglasses and looked for Billy when Alyssa ran over, and surprisingly hugged her tight.

"I just wanted to apologize for all the years we didn't become friends. I know it's not the time to say this, but ever since Billy came over Mom's house to search Mitchell's room, you've been on my mind. The fact is, you've been on my mind for a very long time, but I just didn't have the guts to call, or come over to tell you how I felt."

"It's …"

"Can you ever forgive me?" She asked and hugged her tight again. "You're a much better person than me," she added.

Jessica was shocked at what she was saying to her, and took her glasses off. She glanced over at Billy and thought he was waiting for her. "Would you like to come over for supper tonight?" she asked hesitantly and thinking she would refuse.

"I would love to. May I bring someone?" Thinking of her endless list of boyfriends, and then decided to bring her own mother for a change, and be herself instead of who she needed to be.

"Sure, you can bring anyone you want."

Alyssa lightly kissed her on the cheek and smiled. "Well be over around seven. Is that okay?"

"Seven will be great, I'll see you then."

Alyssa walked down the steps and caught up with her mother getting into the limo since the funeral director offered them to drive them home.

Jessica watched as Alyssa turn around and smiled one last time before she sat in the car. She walked down the steps toward Billy talking with the other officers, and over heard them saying Mitchell and his father were being transported to the funeral home, and the service was now going to be held at the home for both family members two days from now.

She glanced over at a small crowd of young boys who were good friends of Mitchell's smiling and acting slightly giddy. She walked closer wondering why they were acting so strange,

and then, she saw Sue, Mitchell's little divorced whore. Still wearing that tight black outfit she had on with her nipples popping out and every young man was eager to take her home to find out for themselves why Mitchell always wanted to, let's say, trim the hedges.

"It's time to go home boys!" Jessica shouted into the crowd with an interfering voice and a serious look on her face. Everyone turned around and smiled at her, nodded their heads and walked away in their separate ways as Sue stood alone in front of her car, and gave Jessica the evil eye. Jessica smirked at her and looked at her up and down, with disappointment and walked away toward Billy.

"Why don't you mind your own business?" Sue snapped at her.

"Why don't you stop robbing the cradle?" Jessica snapped back at her and touched Billy's arm. "I'm going to wait for you in the car," she told him and walked passed him before he could speak. She looked back one more time at Sue still standing against her car and still giving her the evil eye, and opened the car to the cruiser.

Billy watched her for a moment, and then he saw the same old man again smiling at him from across the street. He stared at the old man wondering who he was, and why he was smiling at a time like this.

"Hey Jess!" he shouted just as she shut the passenger door of his police cruiser. Billy looked back over and noticed the man had once again, disappeared. He looked around for him again and walked to his car wondering. But this time he got a good look at the old man and an image of him sitting on the park bench when he was young came into mind. A slight chill went up his spine as he thought more about the old man telling him and his friends about the legend of Dark Mountain.

He walked toward the car to give Jess a ride home, or back to the hospital to see Paul, which ever she preferred, when Mrs. Needleson caught him one last time. He smiled at her rolling his eyes, and listened for a moment about her getting together with his mother some years ago. He walked away from her without getting her upset, and jumped into the cruiser.

"That lady is going to be the death of me yet. She still thinks my mother is still alive," he said and started the engine.

"Who is that woman?" Jessica asked.

"Mrs. Needleson, the oldest resident in town. Christ she's got to be over a hundred by now, but her mind has been dead for years."

"Then why does she still drive that old car?" Jessica pointed her finger across the street watching her slam the driver's door.

Billy watched Mrs. Needleson in silence, and realized he'd never seen her drive before, or ever. Unconsciously looking down at the license plate on her car, and saw the sticker had expired in 1962. They watched her slowly pull away from the curb, and drive down the road hopefully toward her home.

Billy turned his car around and followed her from two car lengths away smirking and chuckling. He wanted to pull her over and tow the car away, but since she's been driving the car for so long without being caught before, he figured he'll follow her home, and tell her politely not to drive the car on the road ever again, or until she reregisters the car.

Jessica turned around and looked through the rear window at Sue getting into her car. She knew she was in a tiff with her, but she really didn't care. She didn't want to see any of Mitchell's friends get them selves in trouble with that whore, and then have to pay for it for the rest of their natural life.

17

"Bring me back to the hospital Billy. I want to see if Paul is awake," Jessica said looking out the window. She looked over at Billy, and realized he didn't respond.

"Billy, I said you can drop me off at the hospital," she repeated.

"Mmm?" he replied as his mind wanders.

"I said. You can drop me off at the hospital."

"Sure, that's where I was headed in the first place. I figured that's where you wanted to go." He turned the corner toward the Woodland Bridge, and got an eerie, weird feeling inside.

He looked down at the river's edge, and came to realize that everyone that's been dead had been pulled from this one spot. He pulled the car over and ran down the embankment.

"What are you doing?" Jessica asked rolling down her window.

"I don't know. But I'll tell you when I find out!" he said as he looked around the area.

He walked over toward the spot where they found the old man and Vanessa, and looked down at the river and saw his own reflection in the water with his hands on his belt. He quickly glanced underneath the bridge just as he was about to give up and go back to the car. He looked back down at his reflection one more time, only to see the old man he saw at the church smiling behind him. "Billy," he heard his name whisper.

He spun his head around, losing his balance and stepping his foot in to the water. He searched around for the old man, but he didn't find him anywhere. He looked over at the tree where Stephanie smashed her car into, and saw a small metal-like reflection coming off the lower part of the tree trunk.

He pulled his foot out of the water and walked over toward the tree ignoring the feeling of the insole of his boot squishing with every step. He looked down and saw the same piece of metal sticking out of the tree. When he bent down to pull the metal out, he felt a cold sensation on the back of his neck. He remained very still, and looked into the shiny metal to see who, or what was behind him.

"Billy," he heard his name again whisper through the air. Chills ran up and down his spine when he heard his voice for the second time realizing now, it must be the Dark Mountain Phantom.

Slowly he turned his head to look at him. He turned his head further and then he turned all the way around, and sighed with relief when didn't see the Phantom at all. Carefully he looked in every direction waiting to see the legend stand before him, and sighed again.

After a moment of total fear and searching the grounds, he took one last deep breath to relax his nerves. Billy smiled a bit, and chuckled to himself understanding the fact that it was only his imagination getting the best of him. He pulled the rest of the metal piece out of the tree, and threw it on the ground thinking to him self it must have been a piece from Stephanie's car. He walked back up the hill, and opened the door to the cruiser only to find Jessica sound asleep leaning against the passenger door. Quietly he sat in and shut the door, and started the engine.

He drove over the bridge and glanced down one last time at the river before he got to the other side. He glanced into his rear view mirror and saw a log truck coming down the road with its head lights on. He decided instead of going to the hospital, he would drive to Jessica's house and let her get some sleep. He stopped on the side of the road in front of her house and affectionately woke her up.

Jessica looked at him holding a smile from ear to ear. "Where are we?" she asked.

"We're here at your house. I thought maybe you wanted to come home and get some sleep," he told her.

"I want to go see Paul,"

"We can go see him after you get some sleep." He shut the engine off and hopped out of the car to go open her door. Jessica slid out of the car and walked up to her door. She turned around like she was waiting for him to come along, but he looked at her leaning against his car, sort of waiting for an invite.

"You're not coming along?" she asked fumbling for her keys.

That's all Bill needed to hear, and swiftly walked up the sidewalk. He figured since he was here, he would somewhat search Paul's room for the stone, or any clue that would lead him to it.

Jessica opened the door and walked in throwing her keys on the collect-all table near the stairs, and slumped herself up with all the energy she had left. She wanted to sleep, and she wanted to go to the hospital, but she knew she needed sleep more than anything.

Billy followed her up, and quickly glanced into Paul's room looking at everything he could see. Then saw his backpack lying on the floor next to his dried dirt covered boots and jeans.

"Jess, I'm going to take a quick look around Paul's room. Maybe he has the other stone," he said to her and walked into his room.

Jessica didn't care at this point, she wanted to collapse on her own bed and get some shut eye.

The first thing Billy did, was grab Paul's backpack and strip everything from it hoping to find the other stone, but no such luck. He grabbed Paul's dirty jeans and checked every pocket, and pulled out the old letter Paul found at the broken down cabin.

He examined the letter for a moment and had a hunch it was very old, and carefully opened the letter to look at the writing. He walked over to the window to get better light and saw the signature on the bottom. 'General Grant' He glanced out the window, and unexpectedly saw

the old man looking up at him with a smile leaning against his cane. Chills went up and down his spine staring at the old man smiling. He didn't move. He didn't walk away. He just stood there holding his cane to the ground, smiling at him with dark sunglasses on.

Billy quickly ran down the stairs, and out the door hoping to see the old man and talk to him. But when he opened the door and looked over, he was gone. He searched in every direction for the smiling old man when a small, but strange cold wind came across the air giving Billy another eerie chill up and down his spine. He walked toward the door when he saw Shauna pull into the driveway. She jumped out of the car, and walked toward the door unaware that Billy was there, and jumped almost out of her skin.

"I'm sorry Shauna. I should have said something when you got out," he said

"Yeah, you should have," she snapped at him trying to calm down. "What the hell are you doing here anyway?" she asked.

"I gave Paul's mother a ride home."

"Paul can come home tomorrow," she told him.

"Where's the other stone Shauna?" he asked demandingly.

Shauna stared at him putting up her guard. "I don't know, Billy!" she shouted. "I don't know!" she shouted again.

"Shauna, I'm not going to argue with you. I need to do my part in trying to keep people from dieing. We need to work together on this."

"Stephanie went home this morning," she said changing the subject.

"Does she have the stones?"

Shauna ignored his comment and walked to the door.

"Okay, how about if we talk again at Paul's or Stephanie's funeral. Would that be okay with you?"

Shauna stopped in front of the door and remembered Mitchell's memorial was earlier today, and how she was glad she didn't go. But she also knew the chief was telling the truth. Perhaps he is right. The Phantom will kill one of her friends, she would never forgive herself. "Stephanie," she thought, and turned around and looked at him. "What do you want me to do Chief?" she asked.

Billy looked down at the fragile letter he was still holding, slid it into his pocket and thought to himself.

"Well," he said.

18

Stephanie's father sat on the couch feeling depressed and thinking of his brother Lou, and when he died so many years ago. He listened to the quiet sound of someone playing the saxophone on the radio, and holding the only picture of his brother. He took a long swig of whiskey and wiped his mouth on his sleeve.

"Dad," Stephanie said looking for him.

"Yeah Steph, I'll be up in a minute," he said and put Lou's picture and the whiskey bottle on the coffee table.

He stood up, and felt the room spinning around as he lost his balance, and tripped over his own feet toward the stairs.

"Dad," Stephanie said again wondering what the noise was.

"I'm coming Stephanie, give me a minute," he told her trying to get himself up the stairs.

"Are you alright?" Stephanie asked, and looked down the staircase to see her father sitting on the steps. "What's wrong with you?" she asked.

"I'm alright. I just need to lie down that's all."

"You're drunk!" she shouted. "Never mind, I'll get a drink for myself!" she stormed down the stairs and past him still sitting on the steps.

"Stephanie I'm sorry. I just feel bad today. I started thinking about your Uncle Lou when the chief came to your hospital room.

"Dad, Lou died before I was born!" she shouted from the kitchen.

"I know, but that doesn't mean--."

"That means I never met him. The only person I felt bad about losing is Mom." She walked back into the living room taking a drink of water and swallowing her pain pills.

"Honey, I'm sorry about Mom."

"Dad, it wasn't your fault she died. Go upstairs and get some rest, I'll be fine."

"Does your bandage need to be changed?"

"No, I changed it ten minutes ago."

Stephanie's father all but crawled up the stairs, and slid himself against the wall until he fell into his room and onto his bed passing out. Stephanie took one last sip of her water and set the glass on the coffee table in the living room. She walked back to the stairs to go lie down and stepped on the first step.

"Stephanie," she heard her name whisper through the hallway.

"Hello?" she said looking around thinking maybe it was one of her friends making a prank, then realized Shauna was the only one who knew she was home from the hospital, and she went back to Paul's to pick up some of his clothes.

There was a soft knock at the door. "Stephanie," she heard again echo the stairway. Chills went up her spine as she got scared, when she heard another soft knock at the door. She slowly turned and stepped off the stairs. She took one small step towards the door when, "Stephanie," she heard her name for the third time whisper through the hallway. She stopped in front of the door scared as can be, but curious of whom, or what is saying her name. She slowly put her left hand on, and turned the door knob until the latched released. She took a deep nervous breath and slowly opened the door to see who it is, when suddenly a huge gust of wind swung the door open all the way crashing her hand, and the door knob through the wall.

"Hello Stephanie," she heard a voice in the wind. "Where are my eyes?"

Stephanie screamed as loud as she could, and tried to take her hand out of the wall when The Dark Mountain Phantom floated inside looking for his eyes. Stephanie screamed again in fear as her head started pounding with pain. The Phantom pulled his black shroud over his head and smiled at Stephanie as his long pointy fingers came closer to her. She tried to run but every muscle in her body was frozen solid. "Help me," she thought and felt the Phantoms fingers against her cheeks.

Shauna and Chief Billy pulled up next to the curb, and jumped out of the car. Shauna looked at the door and saw Stephanie standing there with the dark Phantom standing over her.

"Jesus Christ!" she screamed and bolted to the door. She jumped over the front steps, through the Phantom grabbing Stephanie away as her hand ripped out of the wall, slicing the top of her hand up and landing on the staircase.

"Stephanie, run!" Shauna screamed. "Run!"

Billy ran into the house unable to see the Phantom at all. "Mirror, I need a mirror," he said to himself and ran past Shauna who was helping Stephanie get up off the stairs. He ran into the kitchen, and then ran into the bathroom looking for a mirror, when he looked up and saw his reflection in the medicine cabinet. He punched the cabinet with his fist and smashed the mirror down onto the sink.

He picked up the biggest broken piece and ran back to Shauna holding onto Stephanie screaming and trying to get away. He put the broken mirror in front of Shauna's eyes and moved it around hoping to scare the Phantom away.

Suddenly Shauna fell hard to the floor, and Billy realized the Phantom had disappeared, and she started to cry hysterically. Stephanie was already in the midst of crying and holding her left hand. She didn't know what happened, or why. The only thing she did know now was that her hand was hurting more than her head. Billy sat down next to Shauna put his arm around her trying to calm her down, and pulled her close to him.

"What the hell just happened?" Stephanie asked between her tears.

"You just met the Dark Mountain Phantom for the first time," Billy told her.

"Give the Phantom his eyes, and he'll leave you alone," They all heard a voice echoing in the air.

Silence grew thick as they listened for more.

"We don't have his eyes!" Stephanie shouted from the top of her lungs.

"I have one," Billy said calmly and stared into their eyes with worry.

Shauna looked at the top of Stephanie's hand, and saw all the blood and cuts on it.

"Let's get this washed off, and put a bandage on it," she said to her and hugged her tight.

Stephanie stood up off the floor, and wiped the remaining wetness off her cheek. "The Phantom, he killed Mitchell?"

Billy glanced over at Shauna wondering if he should tell the truth, and then looked back at Stephanie.

"Yes," he said.

"Then we must kill it,"

"But first we must find the other stone," Shauna said.

"But where do we look?"

"The Dark Mountain forest," Billy told them.

19

After taking time and cleaning up the broken mirror in Jessica's house. Billy poured himself a drink from the liquor cabinet, sat down on the couch, and waiting for Jessica to wake up. He shut his portable radio off trying to forget about the crazy town for a moment, and leaned his head back with his eyes closed. "Silence," he thought. "It's very rare for me to have silence," he smiled and breathed a heavy relaxing sigh.

"Billy?" Jessica said softly standing on the last step.

Billy opened his eyes and twisted his head around to see her. "Yes, I'm here Jess," he answered and put his drink on the coffee table.

"What are you doing?" she asked.

"Nothing, I was just…"

"No, I meant, what are you doing down here. Why didn't you come up and keep me company?"

"I didn't…"

"Well I have to get up anyway, we have Alyssa coming over tonight for supper around seven, so I need to get things ready." She looked at the clock over the television and noticed it was 5:15pm.

"Paul can come home tomorrow," Billy told her.

"That's great! Did you go back to the hospital?" she asked.

"No, Shauna told me when I was here earlier."

"Earlier? You left after you dropped me off? I thought you stayed here."

"Shauna and I went to talk to Stephanie. When we arrived at her house, she was face to face with the Phantom. Shauna saved her from sure death."

Jessica crossed her arms and felt the goose bumps takeover her body. Every time she heard the word Phantom, she remembered his horrible face staring down at her 25 years ago. "I need to go take a shower," she said and started to walk back up the stairs. She stopped half way and looked back down into his eyes. She wanted to tell him how she felt about him, but she also wanted things to be slow, but most of all she wanted them to happy with each other. "I would very much like it, if you stayed for supper tonight and help me entertain Alyssa and her guest. Then after, well, we can watch a movie, or take a walk."

"Sure, I'd like that. I'm going to call the station and tell them I'll be off for the night, and to have Scotty hold down the fort."

"I'll be down in a little bit. Do me a favor, and preheat the oven to 400."

"Okay," he watched her slowly walk up the stairs smiling, and feeling like he belonged there.

He walked into the kitchen and set the oven dial to 400 degrees. He looked around the kitchen imagining him self sitting with her reading the paper, and drinking coffee in the morning. He smiled and leaned against the counter. He heard the sound of the shower turn on, and glanced out the window looking at the next door neighbor's neglected vegetable garden. The weeds had over thrown the tomato plants, and strangled the squash vines turning the squash to a soggy brown. "What a friggin waste," he said to himself as he got the urge to walk over there and start pulling the weeds out, but he turned his head toward the stove and put his hands in his pockets. He pulled out the letter he found in Paul's room and opened it up. Looking at the old writing, he saw the name written at the top and wondered who Major Samuel Har was, and why General Grant wrote him a letter? He read some of the words he could read, but it wasn't enough to figure out why the letter was written. He folded the letter back up losing all interest, and walked away leaving it on the counter.

He walked back into the living room and looked up the staircase wondering when Jessica was going to come down. He grabbed his drink he made and swallowed the rest down in one breath and decided he should make another one, and maybe make one for Jessica if she would like.

"Jessica!" He shouted up the stairs and put the glass on the handrail. Then he thought maybe she was still in the shower, and she can't hear anything.

"Jessica!" he shouted again, and waited for her to respond. He walked half way up the stairs thinking he still heard the shower running, when he saw Jessica walking out of the bathroom in the buff putting on her white bathrobe. Billy quickly ducked down and quietly walked back down the stairs hoping she didn't see him standing there. He grabbed his glass smiling to himself with Jessica's perfect exposed body burned into his mind. He walked over to the liquor cabinet and quickly poured himself another drink. He swallowed the drink down as fast as he could with Jessica still in his mind. "Wow!" he said out loud.

"What wow?" Jessica asked startling him.

"Umm, this ah, this drink is strong," he said covering up his thought's of her

"Pour me one. I could use a drink right now," she told him and walked into the kitchen to the refrigerator, and pulled out the roast she was going to have on Sunday.

Billy turned around and watched every move she made, smiling, and thinking how wonderful she would be as his wife, when unexpectedly there was a knock at the door.

"Honey, can you get that. I'm not dressed," Jessica said not thinking.

"Yeah sure," Billy said and walked into the living room, and heard another knocking noise. He opened the door and looked around. He looked down and saw a small boy holding a note as high as he could reach.

"Who's this note for son?" Billy asked.

"It's for Mrs. Michael's," the boy replied.

Billy took the note from his hand as the boy held his hand out looking for a tip. Billy rolled his eyes, pulled out his wallet, and handed the boy a dollar. The boy still stood there with his hand out and waited for more, as Billy reached in again and handed the boy a five dollar bill.

"Thanks Chief!" the boy said with excitement running down the sidewalk, and hopped on his bike. Billy watched him as he rode off down the street jumping every crack in the sidewalk. He shut the door and opening the note and read it out loud.

Dear Jessica,

"I'm sorry for the inconvenience, but I won't be able to attend dinner tonight since my mother isn't doing so well with the loss of my father and my brother in one week. When the funerals are over, and my mother is feeling better, I call you to make plans to get together."

Your old, but new friend,

Alyssa

"Well, I guess we won't be having company tonight after all," Jessica said coming through the kitchen door.

"No, I guess not," Billy said and handed her the note.

Jessica skimmed the note, and crumpled it up wondering if in fact she's ever going to call, or was that just another one of her lies at the church as she remembered the way she was in high school.

"We can always have a nice dinner for the two of us?" Billy mentioned since the roast is already in the oven.

"Yes we can. Reach down here and give me a big hug and kiss," she told him with her arms up.

20

Paul was watching the television near the ceiling in his hospital room, and counting down the minutes for when the doctor will release him to go home. Nothing was on that interested him, and his eye got heavy from boredom. Paul started dozing off when he felt someone's hand on his shoulder. He opened his eyes and saw his friend Mitchell standing over him.

"Mitchell, they told me you're dead!" Paul said excitingly.

"Mitchell?" he whispered. "Is that you?"

Paul watched as his friend Mitchell slowly turned into the dark Phantom, when he swiftly sat up in his bed covered in sweat, and breathing heavy. He put his hand on the bandage over his eye, and remembered the horrible pain.

"Nurse!" he shouted looking for the button controls. "Nurse!" he shouted louder as the nurse ran into his room.

"I-I, I need to get out of here!" He's going to get me!" he told her.

"No one is going to get you Paul. You're safe here," the nurse said trying to hold him down.

"You don't understand. The Phantom, he's coming to take my other eye." He slammed his foot down on the cold floor trying to get away from the nurses grip.

"Doctor!" the nurse shouted still trying to hold him.

"Doctor," she screamed again and heard the sound of the door opening as the doctor and two more nurse's rush in.

"Doc, I need to get out of here!" Paul shouted in hysterics.

Suddenly a large black man with a bald head, and arms the size of a tree trunk rushed into the room. He grabbed Paul's arms and slammed his body back down on the bed as Paul was unable to move at all. The doctor stabbed Paul with a needle and squeezed the sedative into his arm. Seconds later Paul was dopey, and weakened as the strong black man unleashed his powerful grip letting Paul fall into la-la land.

"Thank you Earl," the doctor said to the black man. "I'll have to buy you lunch sometime."

"Anytime Doc, I was just walking by, and I thought you could use some help."

Paul quickly dozed off from the medication, and never once thought of the Phantom. The doctor put his hand on Earl's arm and walked out of the room with him. One nurse stayed behind hoping everything was going to be okay. When Paul said the Phantom is coming, she remembered a long time ago when another patient came in for treatment said the same thing. She also remembered three days later the same patient came in zipped up in a body bag with his eyes ripped out of his sockets. Instantly she got the willies thinking of the missing eyes and shrugged it off, and then clicked off the light switch.

"The first thing tomorrow, I'm going to help Paul out of the hospital," Shauna told Stephanie.

"What about helping the chief with finding the other emerald?" Stephanie asked.

"We will, don't worry."

"Don't worry? Mitchell is dead, Paul lost an eye, and the Phantom is on the loose. But you're telling me not to worry," she said getting upset and worried for her own safety.

"But if you want to? You can come with me to get Paul, and then after we can make plans with the chief," Shauna told her hoping she'll calm down.

"I don't know. My head still hurts, and I told myself I would never hike up that mountain again."

Shauna put her arms out and gave Stephanie a big tight hug. She knew she was right about never going back up the mountain again. In fact, Shauna promised herself the same thing when she jumped into the big truck. But she also knew she needed to go back up and stop the Phantom. "I'm going with or without you Steph. I need to do the right thing for once," Shauna told her.

Stephanie backed away from Shauna, and started unraveling the bandage around her head. Shauna watched as all her cuts and bruises became exposed. She was in awe. She couldn't believe she even lived through the accident.

"How does it look?" Stephanie asked touching her hand on some of the cuts, and feeling the dissolving stitches.

"It looks, well, it looks good, kinda." She told him lying through her teeth hoping she'll take her answer.

"I can tell I look like shit with your facial expressions Shauna. Don't lie to me."

"I'm sorry. I can't lie to you. I never could. But I still love you though."

"I love you too. I want to go with you tomorrow, up the mountain."

Shauna hugged her again, and kissed her on the cheek. "You can go with me, but if anything happens, like headaches, feeling light headed, or dizzy spells or you just plain need to sit down. I want you to tell me right away, okay."

"I will."

21

The next day, Chief Billy called Stephanie's house looking for Shauna since he'd called her mother's house and was told she has been with Stephanie all night. Billy told Shauna to meet him at the hospital around noon with her hiking boots on, when Paul's mother was going there to pick Paul up and finally bring him home.

Shauna and Stephanie sat in the waiting room for an hour impatiently waiting before Billy and Jessica showed up. Finally the doctor came out and told Paul's mother they had to sedate Paul because he suddenly became hysterical over night. Paul's mother asked why he became hysterical, and the only thing the doctor told them was, he kept saying the Phantom was coming to get him.

"We need to give the emeralds back," Shauna said and stood up from the chair looking deep into Paul's mother's eyes.

"I know we need to give them back, but we need to find the other one first," Billy told her.

"Then let's go find it," Stephanie said.

Billy, Shauna, and Stephanie were ready to go up the mountain, but Billy hadn't told Paul's mother anything what they were going to do, until now.

"I want to go with you. The more people you have to find the stone the better," she told them. "But first I want to see Paul." She walked down the hall with the doctor by her side. Billy rolled his eyes. He didn't want to tell Jessica what they were doing because he wanted her as far away as possible for her safety, and her life.

Jessica lightly knocked on Paul's door, and walked in with the doctor. She noticed he was still a little dopey from the medicine, but he was coherent enough to tell her he wanted to go home.

"Doctor, when can I take Paul home?" she asked.

"You can take him home now if you would like. I've already signed the release form, but just keep in mind he's still going to be in a lot of pain. I'll need to see him in a couple weeks to see how everything is healing."

"Paul, do you want to go home now?" she asked knowing what the answer was.

Paul slowly slid himself off the bed and walked to the closet. He pulled out his clothes he wore when he came in, and slipped on his jeans. The doctor called for a nurse to bring in a wheel chair, when Paul quickly told him he'll walk out instead. Paul finished getting dressed, and slowly walked out of his room never wanting to look back. He walked ahead of his mother, and saw his girlfriend talking with the chief, and Stephanie. He looked at Stephanie the most, and saw all the bruises she has on her head.

"Are you okay Steph?" he asked still looking at her.

"Well, yeah. How are you doing?" she asked him back.

"Shitty, considering I have only one eye left."

"Will get you fitted for a glass eye when it heals Paul. Don't worry about it," his mother said.

Shauna stared at him, and wondered what his eye socket looks like now under that bandage he was wearing when Paul looked over at her, and saw she was staring.

"I suppose you'll run out and get yourself another boyfriend with two eyes now, right?" he shot at her.

"Jesus, will you stop being so negative. You know I love you, so stop it okay." she walked over and held him tight.

The chief started to chuckle a bit, and turned around so no one would notice, except for Jessica. He cleared his throat and tried to wipe the smile off his face before he got into more trouble than he already was.

"I'm taking Paul home Billy. I'll see you tonight when you come over," She told him and walked toward the door.

Paul unconsciously looked down at Shauna's feet after he gave her a hug and a kiss and saw she was wearing her mud stained hiking boots she had on when they went up the mountain. He wondered if she was going back up the mountain, or was she wearing them because they were, comfortable? He walked to the door expecting to see Shauna come out after him, but she watched him leave with Stephanie, and the chief.

"I have some things in the car," Billy spoke. "I thought maybe we would need them when we went up the mountain to find the other emerald. But before we go, I think we should make a plan, and hike the same trail you did when you found the stones. That way, it will be easier and quicker to find the lost stone and put the evil Phantom to rest."

"What do you have in your car?" Stephanie asked.

"Let's go out to the car, and I can show you what I have."

They all walked out of the hospital and toward Billy's cruiser when Shauna looked over at Paul and his mother leaving the parking spot. Shauna waved at Paul with a soft smile, and noticed he just sat in the car and stared out the window like she wasn't there.

Billy opened his trunk, and showed all the stuff he had packed up. He pulled out a high powered flashlight and handed it to Shauna. She clicked on the switch and looked into the light.

"This thing should light up the dark forest like crazy," she said.

"Hopefully enough to scare away the wolves, "Stephanie added.

"Wolves," Billy questioned. "I don't remember any wolves in the dark forest."

"Yep, wolves, a lot of them live in there," Shauna said turning off the flashlight.

Suddenly Stephanie and Shauna looked up to the top of the trees as they heard the loud deep yell echo, and a flock of black birds scattered away from their resting spots. Billy looked up and saw the birds fly away. They all stood in silence for a moment as Stephanie grabbed Shauna's arm.

"The Phantom is near," Billy said. "I can sense it."

"You didn't hear that yell?" Shauna asked.

"No, I didn't. But I know that bastard is close by, I can feel it. He's not going to stop until he gets both of his eyes back.

"Why hasn't the Phantom come forward and take the one you have now?" Stephanie asked.

Billy looked at her in silence for a moment, and thought about that question. He remembered twenty five years ago when he was holding one of the emeralds for three days, and yet, not once did the dark Phantom ever face him until he had both stones in his hands.

"I don't know," he replied. "I don't know."

"What's going to happen when we do find the stone?" Shauna asked pulling her arm away from Stephanie.

"The Phantom will appear the moment one of us has both of them together. But in the mean time, he'll still be out there killing people, and ripping their eyes out to find them. The more impatient he gets, the more people will die. The more mess I will have to pick up."

"Paul," Shauna said quietly.

"Yes, Paul. He's already took one of his eyes. Soon, he'll take the other one, after that, Paul will be dead. That's why we need to find the other stone.

"So, you're telling me Mitchell was holding both of his eyes at the twin rocks, and Paul only touched one, and that's why Paul only lost one eye," Shauna explained.

"Mitchell lost both eyes," Billy said.

Stephanie got the chills in her body, and imagined the gruesome Phantom talking her own eyes. Tears started to fill her eye, as she became frightened for her life.

"But I never touched the emeralds, so I'm safe right?" Stephanie asked.

"Were you there, up on the mountain?" Billy asked.

"Yes, yes I was. Shauna and I both were."

"No, you're not safe. I'm not safe. No one in this town is safe."

"Then let's get moving," Shauna told them.

22

Billy pulled his car over to the side of the road, where Shauna and her friends started climbing the mountain. He radioed to the station and told Sheila what he was going to be doing in the mountain, and to have someone pickup his car on Mountain Road and drive it back to the station. Billy also wanted someone to pick him up two days from now on the other side of the mountain when he radios back on his portable. Unexpectedly he heard Jessica's voice over the C.B. radio.

"Billy, what's your 20?" she asked.

Billy picked up the mic, and pushed the button. He didn't want her to come along, so he released the button, and placed the mic back on the hanger.

"Billy, what's your 20?" he heard again. He reached over and shut the C.B. off. Hoping she'll get the message.

"You ready?" he asked Shauna and Stephanie.

Shauna looked over at Stephanie and cracked a fake smile. She wondered how many of them were going to walk out of the dark forest. And, who is going to be eaten alive from the hungry wolves? "Yeah, we're ready. Let's go." She opened the rear passenger door and stepped out, when they all saw Paul's mother pull up behind them and slide her car in the dirt.

"Jesus, no matter how much I love this woman. She's not coming with us," Billy said out loud.

"You're in love with Paul's mother?" Shauna asked.

"More than twenty years I've loved her,"

"Then why didn't you do anything way back when?"

"Because, it's called being shy. Shh here she comes."

"When were you going to let me know you were going up the mountain Billy?" Jessica asked a little upset.

"Jessica, I don't want you to go," he told her.

"You're going to stop me how?" she stared into his eyes with intimidation.

"What about Paul?"

"What about Paul? He can take care of himself, and besides, I told him what we were doing."

Shauna and Stephanie giggled a little, as Billy quickly gave in to her pushiness watching her walk up the mountain.

"Fine, we're going up now." He looked at the clothes she had on and figured her tight jeans, her flannel shirt, and the high back sneakers were good enough for climbing.

Just then Jessica forgot something and ran back to her car and pulled out Paul's back pack, and headed up the mountain again ahead of everyone else.

"No matter how much I love her. She's not coming with us," Stephanie mocked Billy and started laughing with Shauna.

"Shut up you two. It's not funny," Billy told them.

"Honey, can you do the laundry, wash the dishes, and mow the grass?" Shauna said teasingly. "After that can you wash the floor----."

"Shauna, enough!" Billy shouted.

Suddenly Shauna and Stephanie stopped, and heard the deep loud yell from the Phantom echoing over the trees. Billy turned around and saw them looking up at the tree tops, and knew they heard the Phantom yelling again.

"Hey! What are you doing?" Jessica shouted looking down at everyone standing there.

Billy bit down hard on his teeth growling under his breath, and holding back his thoughts as they started walking up the mountain.

"Jesus, can we say bitch," Stephanie said quietly.

"Yup," Billy said and turned around with a smile. "When she's on a mission, nothing holds her back."

They walked for almost three hours up the mountain nonstop, until Stephanie stopped and sat down on a fallen tree out of breath, and her leg muscles were sore. She pulled out her medication bottle from her pocket, and dry swallowed a couple of pain pills. She looked around the wooded area, and got the sense she's been in the very same spot before.

"Wait!" she shouted for everyone to stop.

Shauna trotted back down to see if she was okay, when Stephanie pointed her finger down toward the twin rocks. Shauna looked at the rocks, and instantly got goose bumps all over her body.

"Chief, Jessica! We're here!" Shauna shouted.

Billy and Jessica came back down out of breath, as Billy sat next to Stephanie, and Jessica took off her back pack and leaned up against Billy.

"The twin rocks are right over there," Stephanie told them.

"Are you sure they're the right rocks?" Billy asked.

"They're the right ones Billy," Jessica said taking a deep breath. "It's been twenty five years, but I never forgot what they looked like."

"Plus, I remember that old sign nailed to the tree over there," Stephanie said.

"Now we start looking for the emerald," Shauna spoke.

"Not yet," Jessica said to her. "The man sitting on the bench said it's where the wolves' food is. Where the hell that is, is beyond me."

"The man," Stephanie said quietly.

"What man?" Billy asked.

"The man who was hanging from the tree we found."

"What the hell are you talking about?"

"Wait Billy, let her explain!" Jessica shouted and saw Stephanie jump a bit when Jessica shouted at Billy, and glanced down at the twin rocks. She wanted to tell them everything, but she didn't know where to begin.

"Steph, take a breather, and tell us where the man is.

"He's in the dark forest," Shauna spoke. "Or should I say, he was in the dark forest since the wolves were eating him when we ran for our own lives. Jessica, he was the man in the paper that Paul showed you. We tried to tell you, but all you wanted to know about was the stones."

"The man that's been missing for more than a month is in the dark forest?" Billy asked.

"Yes," Stephanie answered him.

Billy pressed the button on his mic and called for Sheila. He waited for her to respond, but they only heard static.

"Portable one to base, can you hear me?" he said again. Still, they only heard static.

"We must be too far up the mountain," Shauna said.

"Well then, I guess we're on our own," Jessica told them.

"The cabin is just ahead a little ways, we can rest there, and then tomorrow we can head into the dark forest," Shauna explained.

"Before we go, I want to take a closer look at the twin rocks," Billy said walking down the mountain toward the rocks.

"Watch out for the barbed wire fence on the ground!" Stephanie shouted.

"Billy looked down, and just as he stepped, he saw the barbed wire fence with his foot in the middle. "Whew," he said to himself and pulled his foot out.

He walked over to the rocks sliding his hand down them feeling the crack down the middle. He instantly remembered Lou, Jessica, and the rest of his friends pulling against the rocks laughing and having a good time. He looked down and saw foot marks on the ground and someone's hand print pressed into the dirt.

"Billy!" Shauna shouted as he looked up at her. "Don't say the Indian words! It'll open the rocks!"

"Billy looked back down and saw the words engraved in the stone. He read the words Pkwedano majignol pamabskakil to himself, and still, the twin rocks opened up letting the inhuman stench escape the rocks.

"Oh no," Shauna said and ran down to the rocks.

"Billy, what the hell are you doing?" she yelled. "Why did you open the rocks?"

"I didn't," he told her.

"I did," the old man said standing inside the opening.

Billy stepped away and watched the old man slowly walk out of the opening. Jessica saw the old man look up at her with a smile. Chills went up and down her spine as she remembered him long ago sitting in front of the store, and telling them about the legend.

"Find the other stone, and the Phantom will leave you alone," the old man said.

"We will," Billy said in fear.

The old man walked closer to Shauna and took off his dark sunglasses. She saw his hollow eyes and jumped back in fear and fell to the ground. The old man started to laugh as his voice carried through the woods, and suddenly, he disappeared right before their eyes.

"Let's get going," Billy said brushing off the old man, and walked back up the mountain like nothing ever happened.

Shauna got up off the ground and wiped off her behind. She looked one more time at the opening and noticed the rocks were slowly closing.

"Find the Phantom's eyes Shauna," the old man whispered behind her.

She quickly turned around but the trees were the only thing she saw. Shauna quickly ran up the mountain to catch up with everyone, and this time, she didn't dare to look back, or didn't even want to.

23

They reached the cabin just before night fall. Jessica stepped up on the porch first and looked inside. She slid her hand on the door entrance and felt the wood. She slipped off her back pack, and walked into the cabin looking at all the dust covered items and put her backpack on the table. Shauna walked in after her and saw all the same stuff she saw before, and looked at the black and white picture hanging on the wall. She walked closer to the picture and looked at the man holding the rifle.

"Jessica, look at this picture. Who does this guy remind you of?" she asked.

Billy walked in the cabin and saw Shauna and Jessica looking at the picture, and walked over and saw the man and recognized who he was. "Well I'll be damned," he said. "That's the old man with the dark sunglasses," he told them. "He must have lived in this cabin a long time ago." He looked around and saw the bed and walked over to it. He sat down on the wooden part and felt the hardened pillow. "We can stay here tonight," he said and looked out the door, and saw Stephanie sitting on the porch smoking a cigarette.

"Why would that old man be in this picture?" Shauna asked. Then it dawned on her. She remembered Paul telling her the name on the broken cross in the back of the house. "Hartwell," she said. "His name is Mr. Hartwell."

"So that explains the letter I found in Paul's back pack," Billy told them still looking at Stephanie smoking a cigarette.

Shauna looked over at Stephanie and saw the cigarette in her hand. She walked outside and sat down next to her. "So, she said hesitantly. "Since when did you start smoking?" she reached down and picked up the pack and looked inside to see if it was a new one.

"These are Paul's cigarettes." she said with an attitude. "Shauna, I've been smoking for a while. That's why I knew Paul had that lighter in his pocket the first time we were up here. He also had a pack of cigarettes in his backpack. You never found out he woke up during the night, and went outside to smoke a butt did you?"

"Why didn't you tell me before?"

"I didn't want you to get mad at me. Now, well, I needed a butt, so I said the hell with it. Right now I could give a shit"

Billy walked over to Jessica and put his arms around her, and held her tight. Jessica started to cry on his shoulder after she thought of her son almost being killed, and the thought of what he went through loosing his eye.

Shauna looked over her shoulder and saw them holding each other and smiled. Stephanie sucked the last drag off the cigarette, and flicked it into the dirt. She stared at the smoke still coming off the end and thought of Mitchell, and how he would still be alive if they never came up here in the first place. She looked up and glanced down at the edge of the dark forest as her imagination went wild. She thought of the man hanging from the tree, and the wolves that almost ate them for supper.

"Chief, do you have your gun loaded?" Stephanie asked still looking down at the edge.

"Yes, why do you ask?" he asked as he let Jessica go and walked toward the door.

"Because, you're going to need to use it," she told him.

"Why?"

"Wolves," she said in a low voice.

"Oh yeah, that's right. I forgot about the wolves," Shauna said, and looked down at the edge.

Billy looked up at the sky and saw the sun was going down. He jumped off the porch and walked over to the fire pit picking up small sticks along the way, and tossed them in. He removed the hanging pot, and tossed it over to the side and noticed the broken cross a little ways up the mountain. He decided to walk up and investigate when suddenly he heard a crackling noise coming from his radio.

He pulled it off his belt and pushed the button, when he noticed the radio was in the off position. He turned around toward the cabin and saw a dark shadow walk on the other side. Quickly he ran down to the cabin and hopped on the porch only to find Shauna and Stephanie still sitting on the steps. He looked in the cabin and saw Jessica leaning against the door.

"What's the matter?" Jessica asked.

"I think we're being followed," he told them.

"Followed, What for?" Shauna asked.

"The Phantom, I think he's following us,"

"What do you mean?" Jessica asked.

"I thought I saw a dark shadow run over there," he pointed his finger toward the same way they came.

Jessica looked over and walked to the end of the porch and widened her search. "Maybe you thought you saw something," she told him. "There's nothing out here Billy."

Billy went back over to the fire pit still looking around for the dark shadow, and tossed in some more small sticks as Jessica and Shauna walked around picking more up. Stephanie still sat on the steps smoking another cigarette, thinking of the horror of what lurks in the dark forest. She imagined them finding the emerald, and when they did, everyone was killed including herself.

"I don't want to go in there!" she screamed as loud as she could, as they all heard her voice echo down the mountain and the birds fluttering away from the trees. Then, they all heard the long deep yell from the Phantom echo up the mountain from within the dark forest. Silence fell amongst them as they stared at the forest.

"No!" Stephanie stood up and screamed. "You will die!" she screamed again.

They all heard another long deep yell echo out of the forest, but only this time, it was a lot closer, and louder.

"Stephanie, don't!" Billy shouted and ran over to her. "He knows we're here,"

"He does know you're here!" they heard a voice in the air. "He wants his eyes. Give him his eyes, and he'll leave you alone,"

Billy looked up at the sky and noticed it was getting darker. He started to get scared and looked over at the fire pit, and realized he hadn't even started it yet. Jessica crossed her arms and prayed to God everyone was going to be alive in the morning. She looked over at Billy striking a match one by one, and throwing the unlit matches in the pit. She knew this time he was scared, and walked over to him and lightly touched his hands. "I'll light the fire," she said softly.

24

Stephanie looked at her pack of cigarettes as she breathed a long sigh, and pulled the next to the last one out and lit it. She didn't think she smoked almost the whole pack in just over three hours. She looked up to the sky while taking a drag, and saw one star looking down at her. She decided to silently make a wish hoping maybe someday, she and Mitchell can be together again, and secretly wished it was Paul who had died instead of Mitchell.

Shauna sat with everyone near the fire pit keeping warm, and staring at Stephanie the whole time trying to figure out what she was thinking about, when the noise of a branch snapping in half came from the edge of the forest. They all looked down at the edge, and wondered what, or who stepped on the dead branch.

"The wolves are watching us," Stephanie spoke breaking the silence. "They're wondering when we're going to enter their territory, so they can feast upon us like they did with that man hanging from the tree."

Billy listened to her tell the truth, and looked over at Jessica covering her face to hide the tears, or maybe to hide from the world for a short moment. They all heard another snap from a tree branch as their imagination took them in a dimension of horror, except for Stephanie. She was waiting for the moment of truth when she faces the hungry wolves, and wished upon that star, they would make it out of the dark forest alive.

"I wonder how Paul is doing." Jessica said and put her head down on her knees trying to change the subject.

"He's probably doing fine. Watching T.V. like he does every friggin night," Shauna said disappointingly.

"Or, he's dead," Stephanie said quietly, and saw his mother lift her head up off her knees. Stephanie stared at her for a moment, and lit the last cigarette before tossing the empty pack in the fire.

"How dare you say that, you little bitch," Jessica said to her and tightened her hand to form a fist. She instantly became enraged at Stephanie. She had no right to say that about Paul.

"Jessica I'm sorry, I didn't mean to say that," Stephanie said taking another drag from her cigarette. "I was thinking about the Phantom, and how he kills everyone after he takes their eyes."

Jessica didn't care what Stephanie said, she shouldn't have said what she said. Jessica looked the other way in silence and tried to forget about everything, and to calm herself down.

"I think we should get some sleep," Billy spoke. "We have a busy day ahead of us tomorrow."

"What are you up here for anyway Billy?" Stephanie snapped.

"He's trying to save your miserable embarrassing life!" Jessica shouted and stood up in front of her. She wanted to slap her across the face as hard as she could, but she knew it would only satisfy her anger and cause more problems.

"Stephanie what the hell is your problem?" Shauna asked. "You're being a bitch."

"No I'm not, I'm just saying…"

"You're saying what Stephanie," Jessica interrupted

Stephanie looked at Jessica. She knew she was getting everyone upset, and she didn't know how to stop the anger. She decided to get up and walk toward the cabin away from everyone for a while as Jessica was still staring at her with fire in her eyes. She'll never forgive her for saying her son could be dead. Shauna quickly jumped up, and ran over to Stephanie putting her arms around her. Stephanie stopped and hugged her tight.

"Hey," Shauna said. "We stick together. No matter what happens, we stick together okay? Paul's mother will soon get over it don't worry." Shauna kissed her on the check and felt the wetness from her eyes. She hugged her tighter until Stephanie calmed down.

"Let's go for a little walk. They'll be fine over there near the fire," Shauna encouraged.

Stephanie looked at her through the darkness. From the corner of her eye, she saw something moving fast from within the edge of the dark forest. She turned her head to see what it was, but she saw nothing but blackness. Chills slightly went through her body as her imagination took off. "Teeth," she thought. "Sharp dagger teeth from a wild man-eating wolf," Another chill went up her spine.

"Let's just go back to the fire and stay there. I don't want to go for a walk," Stephanie said.

Shauna hugged her again and shook her head yes. They slowly walked back to the fire where Billy and Paul's mother were deep in a romantic kiss.

"He-hem," Shauna acted like she was clearing her throat, and sat down with Stephanie on the grass. Silence fell around the fire as Stephanie and Paul's mother stared at each other for a moment with a smile on their face.

"Jessica, I'm truly sorry I said what I said. It'll never happen again," Stephanie said loud and clear for everyone to hear and put her head down.

"Stephanie, let's just forget about it, and let it go," Jessica told her feeling her lips tingling for more of Billy's kiss.

Shauna put her arms around Stephanie and pulled her tight against her to give her comfort, when suddenly they heard a loud howling coming close from the edge of the forest. Billy slowly stood up and grabbed a long branch from the fire holding a flame. He swished the branch around looking for anything moving in the darkness. Suddenly another howling echoed the area, but this time, it was even closer. Paul's mother stood up and looked around. Then

Stephanie and Shauna stood up together as Shauna still clinging to Stephanie tight. The wolves rush by them, panting and snapping their jaws. They all became intensely scared as the pack of wolves came closer and closer. Shauna grabbed a branch and lit it from the fire. She too swished around the branch and didn't see anything. Another howling echoed the mountain, as Shauna twisted her body around looking for movement. Barking erupted near the old cabin as everyone turned their heads to listen.

Then, from out of nowhere a wolf grabbed a hold of Billy's leg and sank his sharp teeth into his skin pulling him to the ground. He waved his fiery branch at the wild animal as the wolf tried to pull him away toward the forest, and violently shaking his head back and forth. Shauna ran over and threw her branch on the wolf hitting it on the head, and forcing it to let go of Billy's leg. Howling from the wolves became fierce in every direction, snapping of their jaws at each other and barking rapidly.

Paul's mother quickly grabbed a hot flaming branch as the intense heat burned her hand enough to drop the branch to the ground. Ignoring the pain she grabbed it again and ran over to Billy. She saw all the blood soaking his pant leg just under his knee cap, and started to panic.

"Help us!" she screamed. Shauna ran over to her backpack and reached in and grabbed anything that felt like cloth. She ran back over and handed Jessica the cloth. Jessica wrapped it around Billy's leg and tied it as tight as she could, when all of a sudden from out of the darkness, Billy, Shauna, and Jessica heard Stephanie screaming in frantic as she was quickly being dragged away. They heard Stephanie's screaming echoing the mountain side and getting further and further away.

"Stephanie!" Shauna screamed. They heard her loud screaming again coming down from the edge of the dark forest. Suddenly, it became all quiet. The howling of the wolves had stopped, the crickets weren't even noisy, and not even the logs were snapping from the fire pit.

"Stephanie!" Shauna screamed again, and waited for her to answer.

153.

"Stephanie!" she screamed again as tears fell from her eyes realizing the unthinkable has happened, her friend was dead.

"Stephan--!"

"Shauna she's gone!" Billy shouted interrupting her fearing the wolves will come back from her yelling.

Shauna fell to the ground crying uncontrollably feeling like she has failed to protect her best friend from dangers of life.

"Stephanie!" she shouted one last time. "I love you!"

Jessica stared at Shauna face down on the ground as tears fell from her own eyes. She didn't know what to do other than hold Billy's leg so he wouldn't bleed to death.

"We'll find her," Billy said calmly knowing she was already dead. "We'll find her Shauna,"

Shauna looked up at Billy and wiped the tears from her eyes. "She's dead you asshole! I'm not stupid!" she screamed and put her head back down on the ground and breathed a heavy guilty sigh still crying uncontrollably.

"In the morning we're going in that dark forest to find the emerald, and hopefully Stephanie in one piece," Billy explained. "But I know one thing. It wasn't the wolves that dragged Stephanie away. It was the dark forest." Billy tried to get up onto his feet as the pain pierced through his leg, as he slammed himself back down on the ground. "Wolves can't drag a person that fast into the forest, not even if there were two of them," he explained.

"What are we suppose to do now?" Shauna snapped. "Wait until the dark forest drags another one of us away!" Everyone's thoughts were the same when she said those words, and they all wondered who is going to be next, or who will be the only one left alive by morning.

"Let's wait until morning to decide whether I can walk. Right now, I can't even move," Billy mentioned as he felt his leg throbbing in pain and put his hand on his blood soaked pants,

154.

and then lied down on the ground thinking to himself he was almost the main course meal for nature's ferocious beasts

25

Morning opened up with a sweet sound of birds chirping near the broken down cabin. Shauna had fallen asleep from crying for hours after the forest stole her best friend away. Paul's mother and Billy stayed awake all night guarding, and holding each other tight.

Billy ripped the bloody part of his pant leg to see what kind of damage the wolf did to his leg. He saw the right side of his leg that the skin had been torn down like a piece of paper still attached to his leg. "Jessica, get me my knife out of that bag over there. I need to cut this shit off," he told her.

Without a word, Jessica reached in and grabbed the so called Rambo knife he packed in his bag from the collection of knifes he confiscated from under aged kids before they got themselves hurt. She handed him the knife and quickly looked away, as he grit his teeth and cut the torn skin off his leg. She heard the light slap of his skin, as Billy threw it into the burned out fire.

"Are you going to be alright?" she asked. Looking at the huge gash wrapped with her favorite white shirt.

"I'll be fine. Help me up. My ass is sore from sitting on the ground so long." He reached his hand out to her, when they saw Shauna lift her head off the ground as she woke up and dirt covering the side of her face. Unconsciously she looked around for her friend, and then realized she was gone and again she started to cry. She wiped the side of her face and got to her feet and looked down at the edge of the dark forest. Instantly she became angry at the forest. She wanted to run and find Stephanie, but she knew deep down she would probably find a dead body, or possibly just pieces of her.

156.

"What are we doing?" Shauna asked Jessica and Billy as she looked down at Billy's leg all ripped apart. "Obviously you're not going anywhere," she remarked.

"I'm alright, I can walk," Billy told her. "Not fast, but I can walk. Jess, let's get our things together so we can go. I want to get home before dark."

Shauna pulled the flashlight from Billy's bag and clicked it on for assurance. "What day is that going to be when you get home?" She asked being smart and walked alone down toward the dark forest. She walked down the mountain side looking at the ground for any signs of Stephanie. She saw drag marks from her body, and possibly marks from her fingers digging into the dirt. She looked the other way trying not to think about what happened, and wiped her face with her sleeve.

She stopped at the edge of the forest and looked back waiting for Billy and Paul's mother to catch up.

"Hey Chief," Shauna shouted. "How many flashlights do you have?" she asked still looking into the dark forest.

"Why? I gave you a flashlight already. Why do you need another one?"

"I don't. I wanted to know how many you have, that's all."

Shauna took one step into the dark forest. "Come inside. Don't be afraid," They all heard a loud whisper,"

Shauna stepped back out and looked at Billy.

"That voice was the old man's," Billy said.

"Let's go," Shauna stepped back into the dark forest and pulled the flashlight out of her pocket. She held it in her hand like a weapon for a few minutes before she turned it on, as Billy and Jessica clicked on theirs before they stepped in. The more they walked in, the darker it got, and Shauna finally decided to click on her flashlight.

They felt the mushy pine needles under their feet when they walked. Billy struggled to walk trying to keep the pace, when they heard a faint howling coming from a far distance inside the forest.

"This place is spooky" Billy mentioned as he lightly stepped down on something harder than the pine needles and stopped. "Wait," he told them as they looked back flashing their lights against him. He pointed his light down to his foot stepping on a sneaker.

Shauna looked at the sneaker and realized it was Stephanie's. She picked it up and looked at it for a moment being strong trying not to cry, and then stuffed it into Billy's backpack. She walked ahead again shining her light in all directions hoping to find the emerald, or perhaps the miracle that Stephanie was still alive.

Suddenly she felt something slide over her head as she shined the light to see a rope trap hanging from a tree. "Shit, I forgot about those damn things. Watch your head from these traps hanging down," she told them.

"It's been over twenty some odd years since I've been in here," Jessica mentioned.

"When did these rope traps get set?" she asked.

"I don't know," Shauna snapped with an attitude. "Just look for the emerald, we should be coming up to where we saw the missing man hanging from the tree."

"How's your leg holding up?" Jessica asked Billy.

"I'll be fine if we don't run," he told her.

An hour had past, and still, there was nothing but shear darkness, and not a sound from anything, not even the wolves were howling. Shauna looked around the spot were she thought was familiar as she kicked something with her foot. She looked down and saw the head of the man they cut down off the tree to save their lives. Shauna jumped back and grabbed a hold of Jessica's arm feeling the willies in her body.

"That's disgusting!" Shauna shouted as she wiped her foot on the pine needles.

Billy shined his light on the head, and bent down and looked at it carefully. "Yup, that's the man alright. He's been reported missing for almost two months now. Well, at least we know what happened to him." He shined his light around the area looking for more body parts but he didn't see anything but an old pair of pants near the head. Possibly from the man when he was alive. "Let's go," he said as he stood up and stepped his foot over the head.

"You're just going to leave it here!" Jessica shouted.

"What do you want me to do with it Jess?" Billy shouted back. "Put it in my backpack, and when we get home I'll put it on my mantle! He's dead, let it go!" he turned around and took a deep breath. "Jessica I'm sorry. I didn't mean to yell at you," he calmly said looking back at her.

Shauna walked past them pissed off at Billy for yelling at Jessica, leading the way still searching for the emerald and Stephanie. Another hour went by searching the forest and for Stephanie, when suddenly Shauna stopped. She quickly dropped her flashlight and kneeled down on the ground, and put her hands on her face and began uncontrollably balling her eyes out. Billy and Jessica shined their lights to see what she had seen.

"It's Stephanie," Jessica said trying to be strong.

Billy walked over to where Stephanie laid on the thick pine needles. Her hands were completely bitten off, and she was missing one foot. A part of her neck was ripped off with the skin still attached to the top of her shoulder, and her eyes were completely gone with the blood still oozing out of the sockets. Billy lifted her arm and saw all the bite marks around her elbow and the side of her body. The wolves' sharp teeth had penetrated her skin tearing it off in some spots. She had died a brutal death. She had died in unimaginable agony. She had been left for the weaker wolves to feed upon her later, or she was left for the other animal's to scavenge. Then, they heard a low growling noise behind them. Shauna and Jessica slowly turned around and shined her flashlight towards the noise. The animal wasn't a wolf. The animal wasn't even an animal. It was the Dark Mountain Phantom. Shauna had quickly realized the Phantom had set a trap for them, and knows he wants to kill everyone if he didn't get what wants.

"It was you, you bastard!" Shauna screamed. "You killed Stephanie!"

Billy turned around and saw the Phantom. He stood up and put his hand in his pocket feeling the stone, and slowly pulled it out.

"Where are my eyes?" the Phantom whispered as the wolves ran past him toward Billy, Jessica, and Stephanie. The wolves circled around snapping their jaws and violently barking. "Where are my eyes?" the Phantom whispered louder raising his arms in the air.

"We don't have your eyes!" Jessica shouted and foolishly threw her flashlight at the Phantom, only to see it pass through his ghostly body and land on the ground. Billy saw the wolves' hungry glowing eyes, and heard the wolves' running back and forth panting and eager to attack. He knew the smell of blood was in the air, he knew it was just a matter of time before the wolves taste the blood from his body.

"Shauna!" he yelled as he tossed the stone over to her landing on the ground shining in the darkness. The Phantom saw his eye and went over to grab it. Just as the Phantom came near, Shauna grabbed the stone and ran as fast as she could into the darkness toward the cabin. Billy watched as the Phantom took off chasing after her to get what belongs to him.

"Shauna!" Billy shouted. "You must find the other stone before you can give it back to the Phantom!" Suddenly he felt the wolves deadly jaws viciously bite against his wounded leg. Billy started to scream in pain as Jessica grabbed Billy's flashlight and smacked the wolf in the head as hard as she could until the bulb went out.

Another wolf bit down hard on Billy's shoulder as Jessica was screaming in hysterics and swinging the flashlight around at any wolf close enough to hit.

"Jessica, run, Aaahhh!" Billy screamed as he felt another wolf bite down on his leg ripping its teeth across his skin and ferociously shaking its head. "Jess, Get the hell out of here!" he screamed again.

Jessica quickly turned around to run, just as a wolf had jumped on her back and slammed her to the ground. Quickly she turned and faced the animal looking at its sharp hungry teeth, then she swung the flashlight as hard as she could smacking the wolf square in the jaw. Jessica jumped back up and ran through the forest to find Shauna. She heard the sound of Billy's voice telling her to run, she also heard the sound of the wolves growling and mauling on Billy's flesh.

Jessica kept running as fast as she could feeling her way through the forest praying she wouldn't run into a tree, and keeping her head down hoping she wouldn't get caught in the rope traps hanging from above, when she saw Shauna's flashlight shining on the ground ahead. She ran over to the dim light and grabbed it only to realize it wasn't her flashlight, but the other emerald, or was it the one Shauna had dropped when she had been running?

"Shauna!" she screamed as she heard her voice echo through the forest, and listened for her voice. "Shauna!" she screamed again listening for her answer and wiping her eyes thinking she had just lost the man she wanted to be with forever.

Suddenly she was startled from hearing a loud gun shot echo through the forest. "Billy," she whispered loudly looking back and imagining him putting a bullet in his head so he wouldn't feel the wolves mauling him anymore. Then, another gunshot was fired, and then another. She waited for more hoping Billy was still alive and hoping he was killing the wolves instead of himself, when unexpectedly she heard the sound of barking and growling coming closer toward her. She looked down at the emerald shining and put the stone in her pocket, and ran toward the cabin still holding her arms out.

Jessica could still hear the wolves getting closer and closer as she ran in tears hoping to find Shauna, and the other stone. She quickly stopped running when she heard a strange scraping like noise coming from just ahead. She slowly walked lightly on the soft pine needles still hearing the sound of the strange noise, and hearing the wolves barking coming closer and closer. She saw another dim light on the ground lightly covered with pine needles hoping this time it was Shauna's flashlight, as she ran over and quickly grabbed it.

"Shauna!" she screamed hearing her voice echo through the forest as she smacked the flashlight for the light to go brighter.

"Shauna!" she screamed again pointing the light in all directions hoping to find her when the strange noise she was hearing was coming from just above her head in the trees. She didn't dare to look knowing it was something she didn't want to see. She still was afraid to look but she did look, and saw the horror in her eyes.

"Shauna!" she screamed as she saw Shauna's lifeless body hanging from the tree with a rope trap tight around her neck. Her eyes were missing, and blood was dripping down from her face. Her shoulder was scraping against the tree bark that was making the strange noise she was hearing.

Jessica quickly followed the rope down to the branch it was tied to and ran over to the knot. She jumped up and reached the branch pulling it down when she saw Shauna was being raised higher into the trees squeezing the rope tighter against her neck. She untied the rope and watched Shauna fall dead hard to the ground noticing the other stone shining on the pine needles when it fell out of her pocket. She ran back over to Shauna and reached down and quickly grabbed the stone, when suddenly out of nowhere the Phantom quickly emerged from out of the darkness.

"You are the one who stole my eyes," the Phantom whispered and lifted the shroud off his head and seeing the shine from the emerald. Jessica slowly pulled the other stone out of her pocket and put the stones together in her hands, as they shined as bright as the evening sun.

She looked up and saw the outline of the Phantoms bloody face in the shining green light, and frightfully stretched her arms out holding the stones to let the Phantom take what he wanted. She kneeled down on the ground closing her eyes tight, scared, and shaking like a leaf hoping the Phantom wouldn't kill her.

The Phantom slowly pulled his boney fingers from his shroud and carefully took the stones from her hand. Jessica could feel the sharp tips from his boney fingers lightly drag across the palm of her hand, and then remembered the same bone chilling feeling twenty five years ago. He vigilantly placed them into his eye sockets and smiled widely. And, without a single word, or without the slightest little sound. The Phantom vanished into thin air like he never existed.

After a few moments thinking and preparing for the worst of yet to come, Jessica slowly opened her eyes, and much to her surprise, she saw daylight at the edge of the forest through the trees. She pointed the flashlight down toward Shauna, and wondered if she was strong enough to carry her out. She lightly caressed Shauna's soft hair as the tears fell from her eyes knowing that the horror was finally over and the Phantom went back inside the rocks to sleep. She never intended on losing her friends in the midst of all the battle, especially Billy.

She carefully picked Shauna up and held her tight in her arms like a newborn baby feeling her head against her shoulder, and slowly carried her out of the dark forest and carried her up to the old cabin. She lovingly laid Shauna down on the ground near the fire pit, and sat down next to her to catch her breath. Her son Paul instantly came into her thoughts, as she wondered how she was going to break the news that his kindergarten girlfriend had been taken from him.

26

Jessica wandered aimlessly into the old cabin with Billy getting mauled by wolves still in her thoughts. Shauna was still lying near the fire pit lightly covered with some pine branches she broke off from the trees at the edge of the forest to protect her from the sun. She wondered how she was going to tell her son his girlfriend was dead, and how her friend Stephanie was also dead. She looked at the broken picture of the man on the wall, and thought about everything that she'd been through. She furiously grabbed the picture, and slammed it down on the floor cussing and swearing from the top of her voice as she slammed her foot down on the picture with rage, when her foot crashed through the floor gouging the side of her leg from the broken wood. She screamed in pain dragging her leg out and fell down hard on the floor with tears rushing out of her eyes as she felt her leg starting to throb. "I want to go home!" she screamed. "I want to go home!" she screamed again with her head resting against the floor. She lied on the dusty floor with her eyes closed feeling extremely alone and trying to calm down, when unexpectedly she heard a faint noise like someone was coughing outside.

She lifted her head off the floor and listened again. Another faint cough she heard from afar, and wondered if it was Shauna still alive, or was it a stranger just passing through. She lifted herself off the floor and limped her way to the door and looked out still feeling the throbbing pain in her leg. She covered her eyes from the suns glare as she looked around the area for someone, or anyone. She glanced over to where Shauna was lying and then she heard the faint coughing again. She looked down at the edge of the forest and saw her friend Billy slowly limping out of the forest holding Stephanie in his arms.

"Billy!" she shouted and quickly tried to run down to where he was. "Billy!" she shouted again as she saw him drop to his knees and lay Stephanie on the ground. Jessica dropped to her knees and gave him the biggest hug she could as the tears of joy poured from her eyes thankful he was alive. "Billy you're alive," she said and kissed his cheek.

"I'm here Jess, I'm here." He held her tight as Jessica felt the blood soaking through his shirt from the bite marks on his shoulder and arm. She looked down at his leg and saw it had been ripped open even more, and wondered to herself how he can even walk on it. Billy nudged her away and lifted Stephanie off the ground and carried her over to where Shauna laid. He carefully put her down and reached for his two-way radio hoping this time he can get help from the station. He clicked on the radio and only heard static coming through. Jessica put her hand out gesturing Billy to hand her the radio and give it a try. He looked at her, and handed her the radio without saying a word. Jessica slowly switched the channels and suddenly heard someone talking like they were on the telephone.

"Hello," she said pushing the button tight hoping the voice they heard would answer.

"Hello?" the voice answered with slight confusion

Billy quickly grabbed the mic from Jessica's hand. "I'm Chief William Parsons of the Glencliff Police Department. We're stuck up here on Dark Mountain near the old cabin. Can you call the police to get us some help?" Billy asked.

"Silence came over the radio for a few minutes as they wondered if the person on the other end shut off their radio.

"Hello?" Billy said again.

"Who is this?" the voice asked as Jessica thought it might be an older man.

"My name is William Parsons. I'm the Chief of the Glencliff Police Department."

The radio became silent again as they waited for the person to respond back. A few more minutes went by and nothing but silence from the other voice was heard.

"Hello," Billy said wondering if the person thinks he's fooling around.

"Hang on a minute. I'm on the phone with the Glencliff Police," the voice demanded as smiles were shared between them when they heard the man's statement

Billy and Jessica waited almost thirty minutes before they heard anything from the radio. Jessica became extremely impatient and grabbed the mic from Billy's hand. Just as she was about to say something, they heard the voice on the other side telling them a rescue team is en-route to help them off the mountain. Jessica's eyes filled up with tears and gave Billy a lasting hug. She looked down at Stephanie and glanced over at Shauna still lightly covered with branches. She didn't want to face her son and tell him what happened, but she needed to be a parent, a mom, and tell Paul everything.

The only thing Billy thought about was finding a way to stop that horrifying evil legend so it will never happen again.

27

Four hours went by, and Billy was getting worried whether this man's voice they were talking to actually called the police to have them rescued. Jessica sat alone feeling guilty and crying near Shauna and Stephanie with her knees buckled up near her chest with her arms tightly around them and rocking back and forth.

She stared at them both remembering the first time things went tragically wrong with her own friends years ago. Now she saw another year's worth of horror and has to live with this until her own passing. Suddenly it dawned on her. She wondered since her friends were found in their bedroom lying dead in a fetal position with their eyes missing. Will Paul be the same way when she gets home? "But he's already encountered with the Phantom," she thought. "Did the Phantom go and finish the job?"

"Billy!" she shouted. "We need to go home now. Something is wrong with Paul," she told him.

"What could possibly be wrong with Paul?" he asked.

"I don't know, but I feel it inside."

"Honey, the way I feel right now. I don't think I can make it walking down the mountain holding on to one of these kids."

"I'll go. I'll find help, and then I'll have you rescued."

"No," he snapped with thoughts of her dead in his mind. "I can't let you do that." Billy took a long deep breath knowing she got upset with the look on her face.

"Who the hell are you to tell me what I can or can't do?" she snapped at him.

Billy looked away rolling his eyes. The last thing he wanted to do right now was argue with a worried mother. "Fine, if you feel the urge to run three hours down the friggin mountain and find some help. Then do so."

Jessica looked deep into his eyes. She didn't want to leave him, but the bad feeling she had about Paul being in some sort of trouble pushed her to go. She looked down one last time at the edge of the dark forest, and knew the quicker way down would be going through it. She turned her head toward the two girls lying dead next to each other and walked over toward them thinking of what she should do. Billy looked up at the top of the trees and thought he heard the sound of a helicopter.

"Hey!" He yelled over to Jessica. "Do you hear that?"

Jessica looked up and listened for the noise Billy was hearing. She looked in all directions trying to pinpoint to where the noise was coming from, when just over the top of the trees came a hunter green helicopter moving slowly that had the word 'State Police' written on the side with white lettering.

Jessica waved her arms hoping the pilot would see them as she felt the powerful wind gusting off the propeller blades. She ran back over toward Billy trying to stand up still waving her arms. The pilot spotted them in the clearing and slowly landed the chopper down close to the old cabin.

Billy waved his hands to gesture to the pilot to slow the engine down so they can load the two girls on to the chopper. The pilot looked over and saw Jessica taking the branches off of Shauna. She lifted her off the ground and slowly walked to the helicopter feeling the pain in her leg when she saw Billy limping over to open the side door. Billy waited for Jessica to come closer and then slipped his hands under Shauna taking her from Jessica's arms and carefully put her in the helicopter.

Jessica limped back over as fast as she could to get Stephanie when she looked down and saw the blood from her leg soaking through her pants. She slowly picked up Stephanie as her stomach started to turn when she saw where her hands use to be. She fell back down to the ground letting Stephanie roll out of her arms. Billy tried to run over to help her was more of a job than he could handle. He walked a couple of feet toward her when Jessica picked Stephanie back up, and used all her strength to carry her over. Billy walked closer and took Stephanie and put her next to Shauna. Billy pulled himself into the helicopter and reached his hand out to help Jessica when from the corner of his eye, he saw the old man standing next to the door of the old cabin. He smiled at Billy and waved his hand like he was saying goodbye. He looked down at Jessica and grabbed her hand as she pulled herself up.

"Let's get the hell out of here!" Billy shouted to the pilot. The pilot nodded his head as he accelerated the engine, and put the chopper in the air. Billy looked down one last time at the old cabin, and thought about coming back up when he could handle the walk, and lighting fire to the place. Jessica leaned against the metal wall behind the pilot and relaxed her thoughts for a moment feeling relieved. The first thing she wanted to do before anything else was to see if her son was still alive, and to see if he was okay. As for Billy, he wanted to go get himself patched up at the hospital, take a very long vacation, and hopefully have everything go back to normal.

28

The helicopter touched down at the hospital's heliport where the team of police, rescue men, and news reporters had all gathered around to see the chief and Jessica and to help them in any way they can. Lights from the cameras flashed in Billy's eyes as he covered Shauna over with a white sheet, and to help the doctors slide her out of the chopper onto a stretcher. Billy grabbed another sheet and quickly stretched out the other sheet to cover Stephanie so the reporters couldn't see what had happen to her and take pictures for the morning news.

The doctors wheeled out another stretcher as Billy and another officer slid Stephanie onto it. Jessica was forced to sit in a wheel chair by a nurse, and wheeled into the hospital before she could say a word, when suddenly she saw Doctor Metagaham being escorted out of the hospital in handcuffs with his head down and two police officers one on each side.

"Doctor!" Jessica shouted as they passed each other. Doctor Metagaham didn't glance at her; he didn't lift his eyes off the floor at all.

"Doctor!" she shouted again. She turned her head and noticed the handcuffs clamped onto his wrists.

"What did he do? What did Doctor Metagaham do?" she asked the nurse. Nothing was said as the nurse wheeled her to a small room when two doctors hurriedly came in and proceeded to examine her vital signs, and bandage up the deep gouge on her leg.

Jessica couldn't see anything because of the wall next to her, but the noises she was hearing from all the chaos coming from the hallway was enough for her to jump up and walk out to see what was going on. She saw the news reporters trying to ask as many questions as they could with some of Billy's officers keeping them calm. She looked over at Billy getting a needle

poked into his arm as the I.V. dripped down the tube. Billy was lying on the cold paper covered bed when the doctor looked over at her as he took the curtain and slid it around to hide away from the news reporters. Just then Jessica felt a hand on her shoulder and noticed it was a young nurse asking her to come back into the room so the doctors can finish patching her up.

"I'm fine," she snapped the nurse.

"Ma'am, please. You must come back to the room," the nurse spoke up with a firm voice.

"No, I'm fine". She repeated. What the hell is going on here? Why was doctor Metagaham arrested?"

"The doctor killed his ex-wife," the nurse told her.

"Vanessa? She's dead?"

Yes, I'm afraid so,"

Jessica slowly followed the nurse back to the room, and lied down on the bed. The doctor cut her pant leg off and pulled a big piece of wood from her leg as Jessica screamed in pain. She wanted to smack the doctor for not telling her what he was going to do.

The doctor wrapped a big piece of gauze and a bandage around her leg, as the other doctor prescribed a pain killing medication for her.

After the doctors finished with Jessica, she slowly limped out of her little room and faced the news reporters again still asking questions of what happened when surprisingly enough, a young ambitious reporter saw her and ran over to her sticking a microphone in her face asking numerous questions about why they were up the mountain without even taking a breath.

Jessica looked at him and started to tell her side of the story, when suddenly a tall man came out from the crowd of reporters and smiled from ear to ear.

"They went up the evil Dark Mountain," the man explained to the reporters staring into Jessica's eyes. "Because they needed to stop a vicious curse that everyone knows about, and still, no one dares to admit that it is forever real."

"What is your name," the young reporter asked.

"My name is Samuel Hartwell," he replied. "I was born and raised up on that mountain." Jessica's mouth had dropped open from shock as she listened to the man speak. She knew it was the same man in the black and white picture she saw at the old cabin. She knew it was the man who sat on the park bench for so many years before. She knew it was the Phantom's friend.

Suddenly it was like she and the old man were the only two standing in the hallway. It became very quiet and still. She looked around and noticed no one was paying any attention to them, not even the ambitious young reporter.

"It's you isn't it?" Jessica asked afraid.

"Yes, it is I. I'm the man you're thinking of. I am the man in the picture"

Jessica's heart began to race as she looked over at Billy still getting patched up. She glanced over at Shauna and Stephanie lying next to each other down the hall covered over with a clip board holding one small piece of paper hanging off the side of the bed that read in big letters, 'Deceased'.

"I wanted to thank you for returning the emeralds," the man said softly still smiling at her. "They belong to the mountain. They belong to us."

Jessica stared at the man's eyes and saw the reflection of clouds moving fast over the mountain. The only thing Jessica could do was nervously nod her head ever so lightly to accept his thanks.

Jessica looked around the hospital one more time when suddenly all the noise she heard quickly came back as if it never left. She looked up at the old man and saw that he had disappeared, and the young reporter's microphone was inches from her face. She turned around and limped away toward the curtain were Billy was behind. She quickly snapped the curtain open as Billy looked up wondering what was wrong.

"I'm going home. I need to see my son," she told him.

"I'll have one of my patrolmen take you. Scotty!" He shouted and waited for him to walk over.

"Take Miss Michaels home so she can see her son," he ordered.

"Yes Chief," he replied and nodded his head to Jessica.

Jessica wanted to give Billy a big kiss and hug, but since the entire police department was standing nearby, she just left and slowly limped toward the door. She looked over at Shauna and Stephanie one more time still in the same spot where they were left, and then swung open the exit door with Scotty walking behind her.

29

Scotty pulled his cruiser up in front of Jessica's house without saying one word the whole time he drove the car, and then looked at her with a fake smile waiting for her to get out. Jessica smiled at him, and without a thank you or even a goodbye, she opened the door and stepped out. Before Jessica had a chance to step onto the sidewalk, Scotty quickly sped away and headed back toward the hospital to meet up with the rest of his co-workers.

Jessica watched him drive off with a disappointed look on her face thinking he has an attitude problem, and a personality of a dead squirrel. She always wondered why since that one lousy date they had, he's been a jerk ever since.

She looked up at the house forgetting about Scotty, and feeling relieved she was finally home. She expected to see Paul peeking through his bedroom window, but the curtain's had remained still and she knew something was wrong. She hesitated for a moment as she started to slowly walk up the walkway. Her leg was still throbbing as she thought maybe the doctor had put the bandage on too tight. She looked down at her leg and felt the pain getting worse. She looked at the prescription the doctor made out for her, and thought to herself she should have stopped at the drug store before she came home. Jessica slowly opened the door and stepped in. She looked around the house, and noticed everything seemed to be right where she left it.

"Paul," she said calmly shifting her eyes around the house. "Paul," she said a little louder and waited for his reply. "Paul!" she shouted and opened the door to the kitchen. She slowly limped herself into the kitchen and sat down at the table, and rubbed her leg.

"Jesus, Paul! Are you here?" she shouted. "Where the hell are you?" She stood up and limped out to the staircase. She looked up at the top and knew the way her leg was feeling,

getting up there was going to be chore. She stepped onto the first step, and lifted her injured leg up trying to keep the pressure off by leaning against the railing.

"Paul! Are you up there? I could use some help," she shouted and stepped up onto the second step. After making the painful effort, and almost getting to the top step. Jessica started to smell something strange in the house like a weird smell of burning. She looked down at the door and wondered where the smell was coming from. She stepped up to the top and leaned against the wall to catch her breath and looked down the hallway. She thought about just going in her room and lying down for a while, but she wanted to know where Paul was, and make sure he's alright.

She slowly walked into Paul's room and noticed he was using his small wood burner and making a simple 'I love Shauna' sign to hang on the wall. She looked at his bed all wrinkled up and knew he never ever made his bed, and noticed his sneaker on the side in an odd shaped position like his foot was still in it. She went over and saw Paul lying on the floor in a fetal position. She noticed his other eye had been taken from him, and knew her son was dead. She stood there quiet as her eyes filled up with tears remembering how she felt when she was up on the mountain something was wrong.

The evil curse had taken the life of Paul and his friends after an innocent hike up the mountain. She lied down on the floor next to her son as the tears flowed in streams from her eyes, and lightly stroked his hair feeling his cold skin against her hand. She knew he had been gone for quite some time. She wanted to call Billy and let him know her son was dead, but she didn't want to leave Paul's side, not for a little while anyway. She wanted to be with her son alone in silence, and mourn.

30

Two days went by, Billy finally walked out of the hospital with his body filled with bandages. He hadn't heard from Jessica since she left the hospital, but he heard from his favorite officer she had found Paul dead in his room.

Scotty also told him that Doctor Metagaham broke down and confessed that he killed his ex-wife Vanessa, and made it look like the Dark Mountain Phantom did it to hide his own guilt. He told the detectives he couldn't afford paying her alimony anymore, and trying to satisfy his girlfriend with her expensive taste in jewelry and clothes was getting too hard to handle.

Billy opened the door to the passenger side of the cruiser and easily sat in the seat not to rip his stitches the doctor gave him. Scotty pulled the keys from his pocket and opened the driver's door.

"Where to Chief," Scotty asked.

"Let's just go to the police station for a few minutes. I want to catch up with what's going on around town," he told him.

"I know one thing." Scotty said slamming the door. "You have a shit load of messages from some lady named Allison. She said you gave her a ride home from the Woodland Bridge when we fished out the old man floating in the river.

"Mmm, wonder what the hell she wants?" Scotty turned the corner onto Main Street toward the station and squealed the tires. Billy looked at the guard rail thinking someday Scotty's going to hit the damn thing.

"I don't know, but I know one thing." He said adjusting the rear view mirror. "She came in the station one day with her face full of bruises."

"What, did her boyfriend kick the shit out of her?" Billy asked remembering her long soft legs, and her beautiful smile.

"I don't know. The only person she wanted to talk to was you."

"I'll deal with her later. Right now I have some more important crap to deal with."

Scotty pulled into the Police station parking lot and slammed on the brakes as Billy put his hands on the dashboard to prevent him from hitting his face against it.

"Scotty, I think maybe you should think about taking another driving course," Billy said sarcastically.

"There's nothing wrong with my driving Chief, but if you think I should then I'll take it."

"Just slow the hell down, that's all." Billy opened the door of the car and stepped out, when unexpectedly he heard his name being called by an older woman's voice. He looked over and saw little Mrs. Needleson waving her arms trying to get his attention. Billy rolled his eyes thinking the only reason she was here because she wanted to yell at him for having the garage put a wheel lock on her car so she couldn't drive it until it was registered. He looked at Mrs. Needleson still walking toward him as he leaned against the car waiting for her, and put on a fake smile.

"I just wanted to show you something Billy. I want to show you that I went down to the town hall and registered the car. So now you can take that damn thing off my wheel. I have a lot of errands to run," she demanded.

"Mrs. Needleson," Billy said taking a deep breath knowing he had started an argument with the oldest woman in town. "Don't you think you need to think about having someone else drive you around?"

"If you think for one minute that I'll have someone else drive me around, you're crazier than your father was. Now go down and take that yellow contraption of my car," she ordered with a loud voice.

Billy rolled his eyes again. He knew it was a losing battle with a woman her age. "Scotty," he said softly. "Go to Mrs. Needleson's house, and remove the wheel lock from her car please." He told him.

"Okay chief," Scotty jumped back into the car and squealed his tires in reverse. Scotty slammed the shifter in drive with his foot still on the gas, and laid a lengthy patch of rubber on the pavement.

"Billy watched him sped away in disgust thinking he's going to kill someone someday the way he drives. He looked back down at Mrs. Needleson and noticed she was also gone. He looked around the parking lot and couldn't find her anywhere. Billy became somewhat dumbfounded; it was like she vanished into thin air. "I need to get the hell out of the friggin weird town," he said quietly to himself.

He walked into the station hoping to just go in his office and sit down for a while when he opened the door the phone was ringing. He grabbed the phone like he wanted to throw it across the room, and then placed it against his ear. "Glencliff Police. This is chief Parsons" he said in a snappy way.

"Meet me at the Woodland Bridge in an hour," a woman's voice said and then Billy heard the phone quickly hang up. At first Billy didn't know what to expect, then he realized it sounded just like Allison's voice. He wondered if it was her, or was it someone else. The phone rang again with his hand still on the receiver. He picked up the phone and only listened.

"Sheila, this is Jessica Michael's, I---,"

"Jess, this is Billy," he interrupted her.

"Billy, when are you coming over?" she asked.

"I don't know Jess. I have a lot of work that needs to be done first. Are you okay?" he asked concerned.

"Yes, I just, I just need someone to hold me right now, and you're the only one I want."

"Jess, give me a little while. I'll come over shortly."

"You do know what happened to Paul?" she asked as she started to cry. Silence fell over the phone for a long while. Billy didn't want to talk about it because she told him to help her save her son, and he knew he had let her down. "I heard," he said quietly.

"Come over when you can Billy," she told him and quietly hung up the phone.

The only thing Billy could think of was, when is the funeral going to be for Paul and all of his friends, or is there going to be separate funerals for each one? He knew Mitchell's father and he, were already at the funeral home, but he also wondered if they were already at the cemetery. He hung up the phone and breathed a long heavy sigh. He looked at his office and decided after he finishes with trying to figure out how to permanently stop the curse of the Dark Mountain, and let the towns' people live without fear. He was going to sit down and officially write out his resignation. The days of being a police officer back way then was fun and exciting. Chasing bad guys and mingling with his co-workers is all just a happy memory now. Being the chief of the police is not what it is all cracked up to be. Sitting behind the desk with tons of paperwork in front of him, and making worthless decisions a third grader can answer. He wanted out; he wanted to retire young and have someone like Jessica to spend the rest of his life with having fun. What he wanted was peace.

31

Jessica sat exhausted next to her mother at the funeral parlor holding a tissue. She stared at her son lying ever so still in a sandalwood coffin with painted white roses on every corner she picked out for him. Her mother was the strong one in the family. When a friend or a relative came over to give their condolences, she would usually butt in when Jessica tried to say something and take over the conversation. Jessica got a little angry at her but she remained quiet and kept turning around to see if Billy was coming down the aisle and comfort her. Billy never came over the house the day she called him, and impatiently waited for him until three in the morning. Billy didn't want to at the time, he wanted to be left alone and gather his thoughts about his own life and what lies ahead

She looked back at Paul and started to tear when unexpectedly a tall strange man approached and stood in front of her blocking the view of her son. She looked up and saw the man smiling ever so wide wearing a tall black hat.

"Can I help you?" Jessica's mother said nervously.

Jessica stared at the tall man, and knew exactly who he was. "You're the man from the cabin," she said quietly and squeezed her hand into a fist.

"I'm sorry for the loss of your son," the man spoke with sympathy. "Someday in time, you shall be together with him again." Jessica closed her eyes for a moment as she started to get scared, and hoped the man will be gone by the time she reopened them.

"Who are you?" Jessica's mother spoke loudly.

The tall man slowly bent over and lightly grabbed her mother's hand. He smiled at her and looked square into her eyes. Jessica's mother became scared when she saw the signs of

hollowness in his eyes, and leaned back against the chair. The man let her mother's hand fall down on her lap, and looked back over at Jessica still with her eyes closed.

"We will meet again soon Jessica," the man whispered into her ear and then quietly walked away. Jessica opened her eyes and quickly looked around the church for the man, but knew she would never find him anywhere.

Billy touched Jessica on her shoulder as she jumped and screamed from the top of her lungs as everyone turned towards her. Some smiled and giggled, while others watched on with a blank face. Jessica looked at Billy with her eyes gushing with tears as she reached out to hold him and trying not to touch his bandages.

"Where have you been?" she asked holding him tight as she could.

"I've been trying to get the town back in order." He told her.

Jessica let him go and grabbed a hold of his hand, and wiped the tears from her eyes. She looked over and saw Mitchell's little whore standing close to Billy's side. She was dressed in her usual black little mini skirt, and that tight shoulder less shirt Jessica hated with her stiff nipples popping out.

"What the hell are you doing here?" Jessica said with anger in her eyes. "My son is dead and you're...."

"Jess, relax she's not here to make any waves with you,"

"Then why did you bring this woman with you?" she snapped. "Is there something going on you should tell me before I really get upset?"

"Jessica," Susan said calmly. "I wanted to come and pay my respects with Billy. I called him this morning and asked if he could take me."

"Why don't you drive that piece of shit car of yours by yourself, and stop trying to jump down his pants," Jessica's angry voice echoed through the room full of people.

"Jessica enough," Billy snapped at her in a low tone of voice. "Obviously you don't have a clue of who she is."

"I know exactly who she is!" Jessica screamed louder. "She's the little town whore that likes to scope out the playground and pickup little boys! That's who she is. Now get her the hell out of here!" She sat down next to her mother crying and pressing the tissue against her eyes. She had it clearly set in her mind that the little bitch was screwing Billy.

"Susan is my sister Jessica," Billy said calmly shaking his head in disappointment as he walked away, He sat on the other side of the parlor with Susan steaming mad at Jessica for saying such a thing, especially in front of all of Jessica's relatives and friends.

Jessica's face turned beat red with embarrassment. She didn't dare to look back and face the man she loves. She was so ashamed of herself acting like such a jealous bitch at a time like this. She couldn't think straight, she couldn't think at all. She looked at her son and thought of the fun times she had with him growing up to relieve her anger. Then she thought of the moment she found him lying on the floor and started to weep.

The minister came forward and held Jessica's hand for a moment before he went up to the podium and started his sermon. Everyone sat down and became quiet to listen to the minister and pay their final respects. Jessica stood up and looked around the room skipping over Billy and Susan as she politely told the friends and family all four of the friends will be buried together, and the town has donated a cemetery plot for the memorial stone once it's finished. She also told everyone Mitchell's father will be buried in the family plot high on the hill directly behind the friend's memorial.

Billy stood up and walked toward Jessica standing with her arms down to her sides. He pulled out a piece of paper and walked past Jessica and up to the podium clearing his throat. Jessica sat down and glared into his eyes, and wondered what kind of eulogy he has planned for Paul. Billy started to say his words he wrote down when Jessica's mother was getting upset and

threw out an insult loud enough for Billy to hear. Billy ignored her rude comment and continued to speak.

"Billy, why don't you just sit down, we don't need your worthless speech," Jessica's mother shouted at him again.

"For your information Mrs. Michaels, Your daughter would be dead if it weren't for me," he spat at her and heard the crowded room whispering to each other.

The minister lightly put his hand on Billy's shoulder and kindly told him to sit down. Billy crinkled up the speech he made and threw it on the floor next to Jessica's foot. He glared at her for a moment, and stomped out of the room without looking back.

Jessica quickly jumped up and ran out of the room to catch up with Billy. She saw him slam his car door, start the engine, and squealed the tires as he drove off out of the parking lot. She watched him leave with her hand on the cold window, and wondered if she'll ever see him again. "Billy," she whispered as her breath slightly fogged the window. "I love you." She looked up to the sky and saw the dark rain clouds rolling in from the mountain top. Just as she saw Billy's brake lights disappear around the corner, it started to rain.

She walked back into the parlor room hearing the minister giving his final word about Paul and how God really loves us no matter what we do, when everyone turned their heads and looked at Jessica holding her head down walking toward her mother and quietly sat down. Her mother looked at Jessica with a simple glare in her eye. Needless to say she was telling Jessica without a word to go find someone else.

Susan still sat quietly alone near the back slightly holding a smile, and thought about how Jessica was stuck in the middle of a tidal wave of trouble, and didn't have a clue of how to get out.

The minister stopped talking after thirty minutes and came over to Jessica and held her hand. She looked up at him surprised he was standing there since most of the time she was sitting and thinking of Billy and Paul, and not once listened to a word he said. She smiled at the minister and nodded her head. Jessica's mother stood up, and slowly walked over to Paul coffin. She held onto Jessica's hand pulling her along, and touched Paul's folded hands and closed her eyes as she said her own goodbye. Jessica put her hand on his coffin afraid to touch Paul, and squeezed her mother's hand as she grieved for her loss.

32

Three days later and the funerals were finally over for all of Paul's friends. As Jessica explained to everyone at Paul's funeral, they were all buried next to each other at the Glencliff cemetery with a nice Memorial headstone. Billy hadn't been around at all since he walked out of the funeral parlor, and Jessica has tried to contact him many times to apologize since then.

Susan opened the door to Billy's home on a bright sunny day, and saw him lounged out on the couch watching a Bruce Willis movie 'The Fifth Element'. She looked around and noticed he hasn't been anywhere since his dirty dishes were piled in the sink and cluttering the coffee table.

"I suppose you're sulking about what happened at the funeral home," she said and put her hand on her hips.

"What the hell do you want?" he snapped at her.

"I'm just checking to see if you're still alive. Why haven't you been at work?"

"I took a couple days off."

"Why?"

"Dammit Susan, I'm trying to watch the movie," he snapped again.

Susan walked over and turned the television off and looked at him with disappointment. "Jessica is not going to wait around forever," Susan shouted at him. "Get your ass off the couch and go make up with her," she demanded. "The problems I have with Jessica are none of your God damn business."

"What, calling you a whore in front of everyone is not my business? You're my sister for Christ sakes!"

"No, it isn't. Maybe she's right. Maybe I am a little whore who likes to have sex with younger men. It's still none of your business, so go over to her house and patch things up."

I have things I need to do before I go see her," he said calmly

"What watch some more T.V?"

"No, but since you mentioned it," he reached for the remote at the same time Susan grabbed it before him, and put it on the kitchen table. "Dammit Susan, I didn't invite you here."

"Billy! Get up, take a shower and go see Jess. I'll clean up this, this pig sty for you. It's the least I can do." She looked around the room with total discussed

Billy slid off the couch, and took off his shirt as Susan saw all the old stained bandages from the hospital still on his body.

"Billy, you're such a stupid dumb ass. You're supposed to change the bandages everyday," she said shaking her head. "Come here; let me help you take these things off before you get infected." She reached up and took the bandage off his shoulder and neck. She easily pulled them away not to yank the scabs off, and looked at the bite marks. "It still looks good, but it should be better when you take a shower, What about the one on your leg. Do you need help with that one?"

"No, I can manage," he said and walked toward the bathroom.

Susan looked over at his phone and noticed the caller box was blinking. She walked over and saw that Jessica has called numerous times, even just an hour ago. She looked around and thought about where she was going to start, and walked over to the coffee table and cleared the dishes.

Billy walked out of the bathroom almost an hour later filled with hot steam and a towel wrapped around him. He looked at Susan washing his dirty dishes, and kissed her on the cheek.

"You're coming to Mom's grave with me Sunday," he told her without giving her any decision.

"Fine," she said gritting her teeth. "For you, I'll go." She looked down at Billy's leg as he walked past her. "You're lucky to be walking around," she told him. "That wolf could have ripped your leg off".

"I know,"

"Next time you should wear some pants made out of cement. That'll save your leg from getting torn apart."

"Cement?" he said confusingly. "You have a couple screws loose in your head I see."

"No just a thought."

Suddenly Billy turned around and stared at Susan for a moment holding a big smile.

"What?" Susan asked looking at him strange, and feeling around for anymore glasses in the sink water.

"You just gave me the best idea in the world." He told her. "I need to go to the station."

Susan pulled her hands out of the hot water, and grabbed a kitchen towel hanging off the handle of the refrigerator. "What kind of an idea?" she asked.

I'm going to cement a wall all around the twin rocks up in the mountain, so nobody can ever disturb that curse again," he explained still holding a big smile. Billy was proud of himself with his idea, and wanted to get things started as soon as he could.

"You're the crazy one in the family not me," she told him and watched him go up the stairs to his room.

As soon as Billy got himself dressed in his finest uniform and his white gloves, he walked out of his house without saying goodbye to his sister, and jumped into his car when he heard the sound of Mrs. Needleson's voice calling his name. He acted like he didn't hear her and shut the car door and started to engine. Suddenly Billy heard her calling him again, but this time it sounded like she was sitting in the back seat of his car. He slowly looked over his right shoulder to look and suddenly he jumped off his seat when Mrs. Needleson knocked on the

driver's window of the car. Billy rolled his eyes as he slowly rolled down the window getting ready for her stupid complaints and her constant blabbering.

"I just wanted to thank you for letting me have my car back Billy." Mrs. Needleson spoke. "Your mother will be proud of you when I tell her at lunch tomorrow,"

"Mrs. Needleson, how many times do I have—I'm sure you two will have plenty of things to talk about tomorrow," He told her and put the car in reverse. "I have to go now. Say hi to mom for me," Billy stepped on the accelerator, twisted his head, and threw his arm over the front seat. "That miserable old woman," he said to himself and looked at her standing in the driveway waving.

Billy drove through the center of town heading for the Police Station when he saw Jessica coming out of the card store. He turned his head and acted like he didn't see her, but he quickly glanced back over and saw her staring at him driving by. "Damn," he said out loud as he turned the corner and rolled into the Police Station parking lot. He sat in the car for a moment thinking of what to say if she came over, and then casually opened the door. He carefully slid his bandaged leg out of the car, and onto the pavement. Billy looked up to hold on the door and through the brightness of the sun, he saw Allison standing in front of him. He quickly remembered that she was deaf, and had to speak directly at her in order for her to read his lips.

Allison reached down and grabbed Billy's arm to help him get out of the car. Billy looked at her as he stood up trying not to smile. He looked down at her long thin legs getting his balance, and then quickly looked up at her beautiful face covered with small slice marks all over and instantly the smile left his face as she stared into his eyes.

"What the hell happened to you?" Billy asked and saw her eyes looking at his mouth.

"I need to show you something," she said. "Come with me."

"Where are we going?" he felt her hand lightly slide under his as he walked with her toward her apartment over the hardware store.

They crossed the street and came up to the staircase to Allison's apartment. Billy stopped and looked up at the door and wondered to himself how painful it will be getting all the way up to the top with the condition of his leg. Allison looked at him and smiled a bit. She stepped up the first step and waved her hand for him to follow.

Billy stepped on the step and held his breath for the second one. He stepped up on the third one and then he felt the pain shoot through his leg just like it did when he was at home. He held his breath and made it to the top before he let his breath go and felt his leg pounding with pain. He wanted to sit down, but Allison insisted he followed her inside her apartment. She opened the door as she walked in. Billy looked inside her apartment having his hand gripped against his gun and slowly stepped inside. He looked around the apartment looking at all the Chinese pictures and little knick knacks on the shelves.

Allison opened the door to her bedroom and walked inside. Billy slowly stepped in the room and instantly smelled a strong horrendous urine odor. He then saw her naked boyfriend sprawled out on the bed. He was tied to each bed post with a spit soaked white cloth sticking out of his mouth.

"What the ---," he said out loud and walked over to her boyfriend. "God I hate this shit," he mumbled to himself as he pulled the cloth out of his mouth and threw it on the floor as he stared at Allison.

"She's kept me here since Monday!" Allison's boyfriend started shouting "No water, no food, not even a friggin face cloth to wipe the sweat from my face!"

"Allison, why did you do this to him," Billy asked looking at her and untied her boyfriends arm away.

"Look at my face!" she shouted back at him. "He cut my face with a razor blade while I was knocked out from the pills he gave me!" she ripped open the dresser drawer, and tossed a small vile filled with prescription strength sleeping pills. Billy turned on his radio and told Sheila

to send Scotty and Michelle over with a cruiser. He looked at Allison as she sat down on the window sill, and lit a cigarette. Allison knew she was in trouble for what she had done, but she also knew she would be dead if she hadn't done what she did.

Billy untied her boyfriends other hand from the bed post and pulled out his handcuffs.

"Untie your legs and get yourself dressed before the other officer's show up and take you to the station," Billy explained.

"Why am I going to the station? I haven't done anything wrong!" Allison' boyfriend started yelling as he untied the rope holding both of his legs. He rolled off the bed when Allison threw him a pair of his old pants to put on.

"She's the one who you should be arresting, not me. She's the crazy bitch."

"She's going too pal, don't you worry," Billy snapped back at him.

Billy heard a car door slam, and heard the officers quickly coming up the stairs. Billy's newest rookie officer Michelle walked in first holding her gun in one hand, and her Billy club in the other. We're in here!" Billy shouted and waited for her to come into the bedroom.

Michelle came through sliding her Billy club back in its holster after realizing her boss had everything under control, when Scotty still held his gun straight and forward coming in after.

"Cuff both of them." Billy ordered. "They're both going to the station and answer some questions. Then they're both getting charged with domestic disturbance, domestic assault, and whatever else I can think of."

"That's not fair. She's the one who tied me to the bed since Monday!" Allison's boyfriend shouted as Scotty put the handcuffs on him. Michelle pulled Allison by the arm and turned her towards the window and put the handcuffs on her.

"Let's go smelly boy," Scotty said and lead him to the doorway. "Do you need some help down the stairs Chief?" he asked before he walked out of the room.

"No, I'm fine. Take them away and find out what the hell happened here. Oh and Michelle, she's hearing impaired so--,"

"I know she is Chief, I saw the hearing aid in her ear, and I can talk to her in sign language," she answered.

"Good, I'll remember that for now on." Billy watched Michelle take Allison away, as he slowly followed her out and walk down the staircase.

Billy looked around and saw some spectators watching what was going on, including the manager of the hardware store who was smiling and happy someone finally took them away. Billy thought about Jessica and looked over at the card shop wondering if she was still there waiting but he didn't see her. He walked toward the police station getting ready to cross the street when surprisingly enough he saw Jessica leaning against his old car. "This day is getting worse by the friggin minute," he said to himself and walked across the street still feeling the pain in his leg still throbbing.

"Are you going to talk to me? Or do I have to haunt the hell out of you until you do," she said to him.

"Jess, I'm sorry. I've been busy a lot, and I figured since you lost your son, you needed some time alone."

"What I want is to be with you." She put her arms around him and felt the bandage across his back.

"What about Susan? You called my sister a whore in front of everyone. Is that a way to be accepted into the family?"

"Billy, I'll apologize to her someday. I didn't realize--,"

"Yes Jessica, you didn't realize she was my sister. Even though we went to the same high school together, and we've lived in the same boring town that everyone knows who we are." Billy started getting upset and slightly backed away from her. "I have some things I need to do.

I'll talk to you tonight when I get off from work." He walked away and didn't even look back at her.

Jessica stood there and watched him until he entered the police station, then went over to her own car wondering if he'll ever call or come over. Suddenly Jessica saw a young boy come out of the gas station and thought it was Paul. She blew her horn and waved at him with a smile when the boy looked and just stared at her wondering who she was. Jessica instantly came back to reality and remembered her son was dead as the tears gushed from her eyes while she drove down the road toward home. Right then and there she realized there was nothing left in her life. She came to understand that her life had become full of loneliness, and sadness.

33

"Get the tractor going up the mountain and make a smooth road so we can get the cement trucks up there," Billy said to the contractor he hired to cement a wall around the twin rocks, where the cursed emeralds were kept. He knew the stones were back in their original place, and he knew they were going to stay there hopefully forever as far as he was concerned.

At first the contractor wanted to get approval from the town selectmen's office because they didn't understand the meaning of what all the work was being done for, but since Billy was in total control of everything at the time, he didn't care what anybody said, did, or even tried to do. He was determined to place a ten foot cement wall with no doors around the twin rocks twenty feet in diameter, and two feet thick.

"How long will it take to get the wall poured?" Billy asked hearing the chain saws cutting down tree after tree.

"If we work through the weekend, we can get the road up to where you put the yellow flag. We can pour the wall once the mold is made. I'd say possibly Monday night." the foreman told him. "But that means more money and overtime for the crew.'

"Do what you have to do. I'm fronting the bill on this project."

"Okay, you're the boss."

Billy hopped into his old cruiser and drove down the road thinking about Jessica. He wondered how long it's been since he saw her, one week, two weeks. He lost count since his job, the project, and his new hobby he started took over his life. He decided since he hasn't seen her for a while, he was going to pay her a visit and see if he can patch things up. He drove over the Woodland Bridge and unconsciously looked down at the rivers edge, and saw someone floating face down with their arms stretched out. He quickly pulled the car over, jumped out and trotted over to the side of the bridge. He looked down and searched the water for the floating

193.

body, but he didn't see it anywhere. "This bridge is spooky," he said to himself and walked back to his car. Just as Billy shut the door he heard a soft woman's voice calling his name. He slowly rolled the window down just enough to see if he could hear it again. Billy waited a good twenty minutes before he gave up listening for the noise, and started his car up. He stomped on the gas and flew down the road feeling scared, and somewhat fearing for his life.

Billy pulled onto the street where Jessica lives, and noticed a for sale sign hammered into the ground in front of her house. He parked the car near her walkway, and took a deep breath. He wondered where Jessica was moving to, and how far away is she going.

He got out of his car and walked up to the doorway, and saw Jessica opened the door before he could knock. Jessica looked at him without saying a word figuring he was here on official business.

"Where are you going?" Billy asked.

"I'm going to move into a condo. This house is too much to handle these days. What brings you here Billy?"

"You brought me here Jess. I need to talk to you."

"About what?" she asked playing dumb.

"May I come in?"

"Sure," Jessica opened the door wider as Billy stepped in and noticed everything was already packed up, and ready to be moved out.

"Wow, where's the condo you're moving into?" he asked hoping it wasn't too far away.

"Nova Scotia," she said in a half whisper waiting for his remark and hoping he would say some magical words to stop her from going. "I don't have anything here accept my mom now. Paul's been gone for a month, and I'm not getting any younger. This house has no meaning to me anymore. My mother put the house up for sale two weeks ago. When she sells the house, she'll buy me the condo.

"Jess, I have a lot of plans I want to do with my own life. But I need to finish the project I'm on before I can resign as police chief." He told her and looked out the window. "I'm not getting any younger either. I thought life was going to be filled with a wife, a son, little league baseball. But it turned out to be more depressing than anything after I passed the thirties stage." Billy slipped his hands in his pockets looking out the window thinking of the life he could have had.

"I wanted to visit with you after Paula Sue passed away," she said and walked closer to him with her arms crossed. Why do you want to resign as chief?" she asked with a strange look on her face knowing everyone in town respected him, and would do anything to help him in time of need.

"I want to live my life the way I want. I want to see the states and," Billy looked at Jessica's eyes. He choked up with what he wanted to say, then, he quickly got up the courage and tossed the words out for on last shot at winning her heart back. "Jessica, I love you, and I want to be with you for the rest of my life. Will you marry me?" he proudly asked still looking in her eyes.

"Yes," Jessica said without even a thought crossing her mind. She wanted this since high school. She wanted this more than anything in the world. "What about your sister Susan?" she asked not really concerned.

"The hell with my sister, I don't care what she thinks," he said loudly.

"We're in our forties Bill. Do you think we can have that family you've always wanted?" Billy looked at her with his eyes filling up with tears. "I don't care how old we are. We'll have a family. We'll have a big family." Billy quickly wrapped his arms around her and squeezed her tight. "Tomorrow we start our new life together."

34

The ten foot cement wall was finally made around the twin rocks to keep anyone from going even close to it and waking up the evil curse. Billy and Jessica did make that final vow to each other. The church was filled with everyone in the town, including all of their friends from the next town over.

Billy resigned as police chief and handed the reigns over to his best police officer on the force, Officer William S. (Scotty) Daniels, before he left and packed up to see the states as he so wanted to do. Jessica just heard from the doctor that she's expecting their first child, and if it's a boy she's giving him the name Paul Michael for the memory of her son. Things have changed from the Glencliff they grew up in. Bill and Jessica decided to leave and move south, far away from the mountain they called home for so many years, and to have her family grow up without fear and not ever hearing about the legend of Dark Mountain.

'Glencliff is a place to live,' the new sign said on the town line. Billy and Jessica visited once a year to say hello to Jessica's mom until she passed away at the ripe old age of 91. Jessica and Billy resided in the town of Exeter N.H. just a couple miles from the Phillips Exeter Academy where their two sons Paul and Jonathan graduated from. Billy finished the novel Jessica's first son had started on his computer he found years later in the attic, but to this day he's tried to get it published in honor of his memory. But the old saying is you never give up on what you to do, unless you really don't want to do it.

Jessica never again spoke of the Dark Mountain legend, and she never told her two sons about her first son Paul. She didn't want to; she ended her life in Glencliff the day she left. But the memorial still stands as a reminder to those who knew Paul and his closest friends and what

happened to them. Once a year Jessica still traveled to Glencliff the same day she found Paul dead in his room and plants a yellow Rose in front of their grave. And every year she still sees the same old man sitting on the old park bench in front of the former card store. She ignores his smile and drives by without even a look, but she knows he's there, he'll always be there.

As Billy and Jessica headed home from a visit, Jessica's tired eyes caught the sight of four young kids riding their bikes on the side of the road, and remembered her friend Michelle so many years ago. She smiled for a moment as the thought of her younger years travel through her memory. A tear fell from her eye as Billy reached over and wiped the tear from her cheek with a smile. He knew what she was thinking of; he knew someday she'll be together with Paul so she can give him a big hug. But for now, she can remember her life as it was, and how it still is. Some people have the chance to live two lives in one life time, Jessica and Billy were the few to have that chance granted.

35

Many, many years have past. Generations after generations have come and gone, and the kids are still kids. The old man sitting on the bench started talking loud one day on the park bench for Danny a high school senior, and his rambunctious friends to hear. Danny listened to the old man speaking while he was leaning against the wall behind him smooching with his model girlfriend Kelly Anne. Danny's best friend J.C. walked closer to the old man telling the story about the legend of Dark Mountain.

They listened; they all listened about the shiny green emeralds stuck in the rocks. Danny asked the old man how far up the mountain the green emeralds were located. The old man tapped his cane on the pavement and smiled as wide as he could. Danny nonchalantly walked over and sat next to the old man on the back of the old park bench.

"Tell me more of the green emeralds old man, or I'll be to beat it out of you," Danny threatened and laughed with his friends. The old man just smiled his smile and nodded his head.

"Just follow the signs, you can find them, It's not hard," the old man said still tapping his cane. Danny looked back at his friends with the thought of making the adventurous trip. He looked back at the old man sitting on the park bench and realized the old man was gone. Danny shifted his head around in all directions and couldn't find the old man anywhere. Danny looked at J.C. still looking for the old man.

"Let's go find the emeralds. We'll be home before dark," Danny told them and hopped in the hot rod car he bought from a man he once knew before he died.

Danny squealed around the corner and flew over the old Woodland Bridge heading up the mountain. He suddenly slowed the car down when he reached the mountain side and started to

look in all directions for any sign that would lead them up the mountain to the emeralds. Kelly Anne glanced over to the wooded area and happened to see the old man standing near a tree and shouted to stop.

Danny slammed on the brakes and hurried up the mountain leaving his car door open to look for the old man. He saw an old sign nailed to a tree and read it out loud. "Stay on the path. Danny scratched the top of his head and looked down at the ground and didn't see any path, or even any resemblance of one. J.C. ran up faster passing Danny as Kelly Anne ran up the mountain yelling for them to wait up.

J.C. stopped for a moment and caught his breath as he looked around the woods for any clues. Danny came up and stopped next to him catching his breath and looked down at his watch realizing they've been running up the mountain for quite sometime. Kelly Anne shouted for them to come back down and look to see what she has found. Danny and J.C. looked over toward the way she was pointing and saw a cement wall with dirt, leaves, and broken trees gathered around the bottom. The emeralds must be in there," Kelly Anne said. "But how do we jump over the wall? It's so high up." she asked and put her hand on the cold cement feeling the years of erosion beating against the cement.

"I don't know, but there's got to be some way in," Danny said.

"Over here!" J.C. shouted looking at a piece of the wall that had broken apart from harsh winters of New Hampshire. Danny and Kelly Anne ran over and saw the split in the wall. Danny instantly knew it was wide enough for him to go through and squeezed his body through the wall. J.C. and Kelly Anne followed and saw the twin rocks standing before them.

"The old man was right," Danny said. "The twin rocks are real. Look at these things."

"How do we get them open?" Kelly Anne asked looking around the rocks. Suddenly a strange gust of wind came through and created a wind tunnel sucking the dirt and debris from the ground, and quickly stopped leaving the ground clean from debris.

"Wow, that was weird," Kelly Anne said wiping the dirt from her eyes. J.C. looked down and saw a rock with Old ancient Indian words written on it. "He tried to read the words as Danny and Kelly Anne started laughing, when suddenly they heard the strange voice of the old man.

"Pkwedano majignol pamabskakil," they heard echo across the air, and suddenly the twin rocks opened up and a strong stale horrendous stench rushed out of the rocks. Danny saw the glow of green in the rocks and smiled. He was scared to go in, but he wanted the emeralds so bad he could taste them. He covered his nose and slowly walked in without taking his eyes off the green stones. J.C. and Kelly Anne slowly followed in staring at the beautiful stones. Danny pulled out his pocket knife and carefully dug the stones from the rock and held them in his hand. Without any notice the earth started to shake and smoke started filling the rocks. Quickly they jumped out of the rocks before they closed up. Danny fell to the ground and started laughing about how rich he was going to be with all the money he was going to make once he cashed the emeralds in at the old pawn shop he always browses in.

"This was way too easy," Kelly Anne said looking at the twin rocks. "Why didn't anyone else know about this place?" she asked.

"Who cares," Danny said. "Just think of all the stuff I can buy for you," he told her.

They quickly squeezed themselves out of the cement wall, and ran down the mountain laughing and telling each other what they were going to buy, when suddenly they stopped as they all heard a long, loud, deep yelling echoing down the mountain. They looked up toward the cement wall and wondered what the noise was, or who was yelling. Suddenly they heard another long deep yelling, but this time, it seemed a lot closer.

End...

61193493R00061

Made in the USA
Columbia, SC
21 June 2019